MATT
CHRISTOPHER
SPORTS

The #1
Sport
fo

CHRISTOPHER

ROLLER HOCKEY
RADICALS

Text by Paul Mantell

Little, Brown and Company

Boston   New York   London

First Edition

The characters and events portrayed in this book are fictitious.
Any similiarity to real persons, living or dead, is coincidental and
not intended by the author.

Matt Christopher™ is a trademark of Catherine M. Christopher.

Library of Congress Cataloging-in-Publication Data

Mantell, Paul.
    Roller hockey radicals / Paul Mantell.   — 1st ed.
        p.   cm.
    Summary: Newcomer Kirby Childs overcomes obstacles to find
his spot on a new roller hockey team.
    ISBN 0-316-13739-1 (hc) — ISBN 0-316-13675-1 (pb)
    [1. Roller hockey — Fiction.]   I. Title.
PZ7.C458Ro   1998
[Fic] — dc21   97-33071

              10   9   8   7   6   5   4

                    COM-MO

Printed in the United States of America

Kirby Childs wiped the sweat off his brow, sweeping his straw-blond hair off his forehead. He pushed his glasses back onto the bridge of his nose and stared up and down his new block at the green lawns and tall trees.

The lawns, the trees . . . even the houses were big here in Valemont. Not like in Minford, where he and his family had lived until the day before yesterday. There, the houses scrunched up next to each other on narrow lots. Some were even attached on one side.

Back in Minford, you could sit on your front stoop and watch tons of cars and people and taxis and buses go by. There were store windows to look at right on Kirby's own block, and lots of kids who lived close enough to visit on foot.

Here, if he ever found a friend, the kid would probably live a mile away, and he'd have to beg his mom to drive him over for a "play date." Kirby hated that expression: play date.

"Mom!" Kirby shouted, knowing she could hear him through the screen door. She was unpacking boxes in the dining room.

"What is it, honey?" his mother's tired but cheerful voice rang out.

"Could you bring me a lemonade or a soda or something?"

There was a distinct moment of silence, then, "Kirby, I'm working very hard. You can get up and get your own drink. And if you're bored, I could use some muscle power."

Kirby got up and went inside, dragging his feet with every step. Why did it have to be so hot? Why weren't there any kids around here? It was the end of June, and school had just gotten out.

They couldn't *all* have gone off to summer camp, could they?

That's where his mom had said they'd gone. She'd been to Valemont a lot over the past couple of weeks, and she'd met the neighbors and everything. She said they were very nice, but all their kids were in camp or visiting relatives. Stuff like that.

Kirby's mom had her head buried in a box and was fishing things out onto the dining room floor. He went past her and into the kitchen. He knew he shouldn't have asked her to get him a drink. He knew he should be helping her. But why did they have to come here to Valemont, anyway? What was so wrong with Minford?

He poured himself a lemonade and started wandering back toward the dining room. Catching sight of himself in the hallway mirror, Kirby paused to fix his hair and his glasses — which were hanging crooked, as usual.

Kirby wished he were taller. He was thirteen,

but everyone said he looked eleven. He was too skinny, and his dad was always telling him to stand up straight. Kirby tried it in the mirror. He still looked short, no matter what. His parents kept telling him he was going to start his "growth spurt" anytime now. Kirby sure wished that time would come soon. He was tired of being made fun of.

An idea hit him, and Kirby went back and got his mom a lemonade, too. "Here, Mom," he said, handing it to her.

His mom took it and gave him a big smile. Kirby thought his mother was one of the prettiest ladies he'd ever seen. She kind of hid it, the way she dressed and didn't use makeup. But she couldn't hide her huge blue eyes and her blond hair. Kirby had the same hair, but he didn't like it on him. It was girl's hair, all the way.

"Thanks," his mom said. "Now, that's what I call help!"

"When is Dad getting home?" Kirby sat down

on the floor next to her and took a gulp of lemonade.

"Not for another couple of hours. Daddy's an executive now. They have to work long hours sometimes."

"I know. You already told me. Does that mean he's going to be home late for dinner every night?"

"Of course not, Kirby. But sometimes, yes."

Kirby's mom had worked as a therapist in Minford. She was going to work here in Valemont, too, eventually. But first she had to get a bunch of new clients. In the meantime, she'd be around a lot. But Kirby knew she'd be too busy fixing up the house to pay much attention to him.

"Whatcha thinking?" she asked him, giving him that penetrating look of hers. Sometimes Kirby wished his mom wasn't a therapist. Maybe then she wouldn't be so interested in what he was thinking and feeling all the time.

"How come all the kids here go to camp?" he asked.

"Oh, so that's it. I kinda figured." His mom put an arm around his shoulders and gave him a squeeze. "You'll get to know people sooner or later. It's just going to be tough for a little while until you do."

"I guess . . ."

"You know, it might do you good to get some physical activity, honey."

Kirby rolled his eyes. "It's too hot, Mom," he said.

"Well, it's going to be hot all summer, so if that's your excuse, you might as well go to bed now and stay there till school starts," his mom joked.

"What am I supposed to do?" Kirby complained.

"You're a good athlete," his mom replied. "Maybe there's a ball game going on somewhere."

"Baseball takes eighteen kids, Mom," Kirby reminded her.

"How about basketball?"

"Not my sport," Kirby shot back. "Maybe after my growth spurt."

His mom had to laugh at that one. "A natural-born comedian," she said, shaking her head. "Okay, how about tennis? They have some good courts down by the park."

Kirby sighed. "Tennis is okay, but I feel stupid going over there and waiting around to find someone to play with. It's kind of pathetic, you know?"

"Mmmm," his mom said, nodding. "I guess I can understand the feeling. It must be hard, being the only kid around and not knowing anybody. But you know, if you get on your bike and take a ride around, you never know who or what you might find."

"My bike's at the store back in Minford, getting fixed, remember?" Kirby said.

"Oh, no — that's right!" his mother recalled. "I'm sorry, honey. I forgot to pick it up. I'll have to go back over the weekend and get it. But hey — what about your skates? You could explore that way."

Kirby thought about it for a minute. He didn't

really feel like putting out all that energy for nothing. But he guessed it was better than hanging around and risking being put to work. "Okay," he said. "Where are they?"

"In the big box in the garage," she told him. "Have fun, okay? Stick to the sidewalks and be back by suppertime."

"I will," Kirby assured her on his way out the door. "I'll probably just go around the block a few times."

But as he headed up the driveway, he spied a Valemont street map on the front seat of the car. Might as well take that along, he thought. Maybe I'll find some kids in one of these other neighborhoods. Reaching through the open car window, he grabbed the map and tucked it into his pocket.

He went into the garage and found his skates, then sat there in the cool stillness lacing them up and putting on all his protective gear: helmet, elbow pads, knee pads, wrist guards. Then he opened the garage door with the neat electronic opener (there were *some* things that were better here) and skated off down the block.

It was true what his mom had said, he reflected as he pumped his legs to gain speed. He was a good all-around athlete. He figured that if Valemont was like Minford, where the people you played sports with were the ones you hung out with, too, he'd wind up having enough friends eventually.

The problem was this summer. It was going to feel like forever unless he found somebody to do things with.

After checking the map, he headed in the direction of downtown, which was about two miles away. Avoiding the main road, he went past block after block of big, stately homes. Many of them had swing sets in the backyards, but he didn't see a kid over five on any of them. Nobody was biking in the street, or skating, or playing basketball in their driveway, or taking their dog for a walk.

Maybe my folks will let me have a dog now that

we live here, he thought. Then he remembered his dad's allergy to animal fur. Kirby might be able to talk him into getting a fish or a parakeet, but that wasn't the same as having a dog, now, was it?

About halfway downtown, Kirby passed a row of small stores. In front of one, a grocery, two boys were sitting on the curb, drinking sodas. One was wearing mirrored sunglasses and had headphones on, connected to a CD player strapped to his belt. He was nodding to the music. The other was bareheaded, with a buzz cut. He was looking up and down the street, squinting in the bright sunlight. They seemed to be a year or two older than Kirby, but he figured he'd try introducing himself anyway. After all, it looked like they were the only three kids in town. Kirby skated over and said "Hey" to the buzz cut.

Bad idea. The kid just looked Kirby up and down, chewing like he had gum in his mouth, then turned his head and spat on the curb.

"Geek," he muttered, and jabbed his pal in the arm.

The kid in shades looked up at Kirby and kept looking at him, not moving, not smiling.

Kirby backed off. "Never mind," he said. "Forget it."

"Forget what, geek?" Buzz Cut called after him. Kirby ignored him, and went on skating toward downtown.

Great, he thought. If everyone in Valemont is as friendly as those two, I'm going to be Mr. Popularity.

He thought about turning around and going back home, but he wanted to be able to say to his mom, "I looked everywhere, and there was nobody." Besides, if he turned back now, he'd have to pass by those two again.

Thanks, but no thanks, he said to himself.

As he passed the corner of E Street, he was thinking it was only ten more blocks to the town square. There was an air-conditioned sandwich shop there. He remembered it from the day they'd come looking at houses. He could go there and cool off, maybe get an ice cream soda or something.

He was fishing in his pockets to see if he'd brought any money with him when he heard a boy's voice to his right shouting, "He shoots . . . he scores!"

Kirby turned and felt his heart leap — there, in the middle of E Street, about half a block away, was a bunch of kids playing hockey on skates!

Like a wanderer in the desert who sees an oasis of cool water, Kirby raced toward them, hoping they weren't a mirage.

2

Shoot the puck! Shoot the puck!"

Kirby skated to a halt, a couple of houses short of where the kids were playing, and leaned up against a big old tree.

"Ow!" cried the goalie as the shot struck his mask and ricocheted away.

"Aw, come on — that's what masks are for," the shooter called out.

"You try it," the goalie replied. He whipped off his mask and offered it to the shooter. Billowing brown hair tumbled down the goalie's shoulders. "He" was a girl!

"Come on, Lainie," said one of the other players. "Just stay in goal for a few more minutes."

"Why can't I do some shooting and one of you

guys play goalie?" Lainie complained.

"Because," a third boy explained, "you're our goalie for the games. If you don't practice, how are you gonna get better?"

"Well, it's hot under here." Lainie put the mask back on. "I hope you all appreciate that."

They went back to their practice, and Kirby sat down on the curb to watch. There were five of them in all. Two were playing forward, shooting the puck at Lainie after passing it back and forth between them. Two were on defense, trying to prevent the first two from getting off a shot.

Lainie stood in front of the net, guarding it with her goalie stick. She was in full getup, with big, flat-fronted leg pads and arm pads. There was plastic armor under her white uniform, which had a red number 1 on it. And of course, there was the big monster mask that protected her head and face, and hid the fact that she was a girl. No wonder she was too hot.

Lainie was tall — kind of cute, Kirby thought,

but also kind of tough. He thought she was pretty cool, too — stopping all those shots the guys were firing at her. Back in Minford, none of the girls played any sports with the boys. Not once they were ten or eleven, anyway. But Lainie, taller than any of the boys, was stopping most of their shots without much of a problem. She was definitely an athlete, Kirby decided.

The boys, all four of them, were also wearing white uniforms with numbers on them. He couldn't tell what they looked like, really, not with their helmets on. Theirs had clear Plexiglas face guards, while Lainie's goalie mask was much bulkier and had red metal bars across the face for protection.

The two boys on offense seemed like real athletes, too. They were well built and fast on their skates. The defenders, though, were not as good. One was overweight. That was obvious to Kirby, even through the kid's loose-fitting jersey. The other would trip over his own skates every once in a while, and his stick would go flailing out as he tried to keep from falling. Kirby felt sorry for him. It must be awful to be klutzy, he thought ruefully. Almost as bad as being short.

Kirby noticed, however, that nobody seemed to make fun of the clumsy boy. These kids all seemed to like each other.

"Oh, nice feed, Trevor!" one forward told the other after his pass flew way wide and into the bushes. "Wanna go get that?"

Kirby giggled softly. That was how he and his friends all used to talk to each other back in Minford.

"Comin' at you!"

Trevor grabbed a second puck, then reared his stick back and sent a slap shot screaming toward the goal mouth. Lainie flinched as the puck hit the goalpost and ricocheted away. On its side, the puck rolled and rolled, as the other forward gave chase. It rolled until it came to a stop at the curb, right between Kirby's skates.

Kirby looked down at it. Then he looked up at the forward, who wore number 14 on his jersey, with the letter C by his left shoulder. Kirby guessed that this boy was the team captain.

The kid was standing over Kirby, reaching out his hand. For a second, Kirby stared at it — was he offering his hand to shake?

"Puck, please?" the boy prodded. Kirby turned red in the face, then grabbed the puck and handed it to the kid, who skated away with it.

Kirby shook his head, feeling stupid. That kid must have thought he was a total geek! Good thing Kirby hadn't actually tried to shake his hand — that would have been a total disaster.

"Forget it," he heard Lainie say. "I'm taking a break. Shoot at an empty net for a while."

The others groaned and complained, but seeing that Lainie meant what she'd said, they dropped the puck and started trying to steal it from each other.

Lainie skated toward Kirby. Then she veered toward the curb, where she'd left her gray equipment bag. She fished a bottle of blue sports drink out of it, then sat down on the curb to drink it, placing her mask, blocking pad, gloves, and goalie stick on the grass next to her.

Kirby watched her. Well, he thought, if I'm going to make friends, now is as good a time as any. He got up and skated over to her. "Hi," he said.

Lainie looked him over and gave him a quick smile. "Hi," she replied. "Who're you?"

"Kirby Childs," he said.

"I'm Lainie Gifford," she told him. "So you're on skates, huh?"

"Yeah." He nodded, not sure what to say next.

"So sit down," she told him. He did, moving some of Lainie's equipment aside.

"I just moved here day before yesterday," Kirby said, trying to explain what he was doing there.

"Where do you live?"

"Over on Oliver Street."

"Way the other end of town?" That got her attention. "Why'd you skate all the way over here?"

"There aren't any kids where I live. They're all at camp and stuff — or else they're inside, watching TV or playing video games or something — I don't know." Kirby sighed.

"I know what you mean. My parents wanted me to go to camp, too, but they didn't get the paperwork done in time and there wasn't any space left. So here I am."

"What's so great about camp, anyway?" Kirby volunteered. "I like to be home."

"Yeah? Where'd you live before this?" Lainie asked.

"Minford."

"How do you like Valemont so far?"

"It's okay, I guess. Minford was better, though."

"Oh, yeah?"

"Well, there were lots of kids around during the summer, and they had an ice hockey rink."

"Sounds cool. I've never been to Minford." Lainie took a swig of her sports drink and wiped the sweat from her forehead.

"What grade are you going into? Ninth?" Kirby asked.

Lainie smiled. "No, eighth. I'm thirteen."

"Really? Me, too!"

"You're thirteen?" Lainie said. She sounded surprised.

"I know, I look eleven, right?" Kirby sighed again and looked down at the ants crawling in the street.

"No, I guess you could be thirteen," Lainie said generously. "It's just that —"

"I know. I'm short, right?"

"Well, no offense, but you are."

"I know. It bites."

"Hey, you think being taller than all the boys in your class is fun? I'll trade you." She smiled.

Kirby smiled back. "I wish," he said.

"Hey, Kirby, you play hockey?" she asked.

"I've played ice hockey," he replied. "Goalie, actually."

"Good!" Lainie clapped him on the back. "Hey, you guys!" she shouted. "I found us another goalie!"

"Oh, no, wait a minute," Kirby quickly objected. "I've never played hockey on in-line skates . . . and I'm not —"

"All right!" number 14 said, skating up to Kirby and Lainie. "Who's my next victim?"

"Ha, ha, Marty. This is Kirby. He's new in town. Take it easy on him, okay?"

"Hey, Kirby," he said. "I'm Marty. You really wanna get in there and try to stop my famous slap shot?"

"Actually —"

"Yes, he does!" Lainie interrupted him before Kirby could say no. "Here, we'll tighten up the mask and gear for you. Man, I've been waiting forever for a chance to play forward!"

"Hey, Nick! Trev! Jamal! Check out the new goalie!"

"All right! Excellent!" came the shouts of approval, mixed with laughter as Kirby stood there, decked out in goalie gear that was way too big for him.

"Let's get ready to rum-bull!" Marty yelled, and they all got up to shoot the puck at Kirby.

Kirby stood there in front of the goal, feeling terrified. This was it — this was his big chance.

If he flopped, would they ever want to be friends with him?

Zing! A shot winged at him before he even knew it was coming. Kirby raised his arm to protect himself — and miraculously, the puck caromed off his catch glove!

"Nice save, Kelly!" Marty said.

"Kirby. It's Kirby," Kirby said.

"Get it right," Lainie demanded, and took a pretty good shot at Kirby herself.

"Kirby, whatever," Marty said good-naturedly, getting the rebound. "Hey, Kirby — curb this one!" And he fired a bullet at the goal, low and to the left.

Kirby dropped to the ground, his legs splayed out in a split. It hurt like crazy — he hadn't warmed up at all — but his left leg pad smothered the puck.

"Not bad, for a little dude," the other forward said to Marty. "Of course, with your wimpy shot . . ."

"Be quiet, Trevor," Marty said. "Let's see if you can get one past him."

"All right," Trevor said, accepting the challenge and taking the puck from Marty's stick. "Here you go, goalie!" He skated three steps closer to the goal, wound up in full flight, and fired.

The puck was past Kirby when he instinctively flashed his catch glove out and grabbed it.

"Score! Score!" Trevor shouted. "It was past the goal mouth!"

"Never mind. That was some save," Marty said, skating over to Kirby. "What did you say your name was?" he asked, interested this time.

"Kirby. Kirby Childs."

"You're how old?"

"Thirteen."

"Get out."

"Seriously."

"Okay, whatever you say. Listen, Kirby, can you skate and shoot, too?"

"Uh-huh. I think so. When I used to play ice hockey, I was mostly a goalie, but I scored two goals the one time they let me play forward. Then they put me back in goal. They thought I was too small to play forward. Like I might get hurt or something." He rolled his eyes to show what he thought of *that*.

"Yeah. Except we've already got a goalie." Lainie was standing there, with her hands on her hips. "Me. Remember?" Staring at Marty in annoyance, she yanked the stick out of Kirby's hands. Kirby took off the mask and handed it back to her, too.

"I thought you were too hot and sweaty under the mask and all that gear," Marty said, rubbing it in.

"You know I could have stopped those wimpy shots just as well as Kirby," she said hotly.

"She could have, too," Kirby agreed. He didn't want to get Lainie mad at him. She was the first friend he'd made here in Valemont.

"Thanks," Lainie said in a calmer tone. "Why

don't you give him a shot at forward, Bledsoe? I'll get back in goal."

"Next time," Marty said. "I've gotta get home for dinner."

"Oh, no — me, too!" Kirby said. "What time is it?"

"Five forty-five," the overweight defenseman said, checking his watch. "I'd better head out, too. Same time tomorrow?"

"Four o'clock, Nick," Marty agreed. Then he turned to Kirby. "Wanna join us?"

"I'll be here!" Kirby said excitedly.

"Cool," Marty said. "See you then, little guy."

The boys all skated away in the other direction, but Lainie was going a couple of blocks in Kirby's direction.

"So, you guys just get together to practice?" Kirby asked.

"No way! We're a team — the E Street Skates!" Lainie said proudly. "See the uniforms?"

"Pretty cool. Who do you play against?" Kirby asked.

"There's only one other team in town," she told him. "The Bates Avenue Bad Boys. We hate them, and they hate us. Once every week or two, we get together for a game."

"Who wins?"

"Mostly them. But we're getting better. Hey, we just got ourselves a new player, didn't we?"

Kirby beamed as she waved and skated off down G Street, toting her big gray gear bag over her shoulder. "See you tomorrow!" she called.

"Bye!"

Kirby skated for home, filled with energy and excitement. Living in Valemont isn't going to be so bad after all, he thought hopefully.

Just then, he skated by the row of stores he'd passed on the way there. Those two mean kids had gone. Kirby looked up at the street sign on the corner.

"Bates Avenue," he said under his breath. "Uh-oh."

3

Kirby got home, tired and sweaty, just moments after the church bells in town all rang six o'clock. "Mom!" he called out as he plumped down on the front steps and began unlacing his skates. "I'm home!"

"Hi, Kirby!" It was his father's voice instead, coming through the open screen door. He sat down next to Kirby and put an arm around his shoulders. "How was your day, son?"

"Great!" Kirby said, pulling off his helmet and starting on his elbow pads. "I met these kids, and —"

"That's terrific," his dad interrupted, giving him a squeeze. "I knew you'd get into the swing of things."

Kirby's dad had straight blond hair, like his own, except that his dad's hung straight down, while Kirby's tended to stick up. His mom's hair was like that, too. His dad also wore wire-rim glasses, was skinny, had blue eyes, and was a worrier. That was the only bad part about him.

Kirby washed up quickly, then came down when his mom rang the bell for dinner. The Childs family had always done that — Kirby's great-great-grandparents had probably rung a dinner bell, too.

Earlier that day, Kirby had been wishing he had a brother or a sister, like so many of his friends back in Minford. Being an only child was okay, because you didn't have to share any of your stuff. On the other hand, it could be lonely when none of your friends was available. Of course, now that he'd met the E Street Skates, that didn't matter anymore. He was going to be all set for the summer.

Dinner was ravioli — Kirby's favorite, with broccoli, one of the few green vegetables he was usually willing to eat, and mint chip ice cream for dessert. Clearly his mom had gone to the trouble of making foods he liked for their first dinner in their new home.

As they were eating, Mr. Childs told them all about his first day at his new job. "It's quiet up there in that office," he said. "Not like down on the plant floor, where I used to be, back in Minford. I think I could get used to this." He seemed really happy about things at work.

Good, Kirby thought. Because he had a really big favor to ask both his parents.

"So, Kirby, what did you discover on your skates this afternoon?" his mom finally asked as they were finishing dessert. "Did you meet any kids?"

"He sure did!" his dad said. "First words I got out of him when he came home."

"Dad," Kirby said, rolling his eyes. His dad was always doing that — answering for him. "She asked me, not you."

"Oh. Sorry," his dad said, wiping his mouth

with a napkin. "Didn't mean to interrupt. Go on with what you were about to say." Kirby could tell his dad was smiling under the napkin. It irritated him. His parents still thought he was a little kid.

"Anyway, these kids were playing in-line hockey, and they let me play with them. I did really well, too — I was in goal, and I stopped all of their shots . . . well, except one. They call themselves the E Street Skates, and the best thing is, they said I can practice with them again tomorrow."

"E Street?" his father echoed. "You went all the way over to E Street?"

"Kirby, you told me you were just going around the block," his mother chided. "If I had known you were planning to skate all the way over there, I don't think I would have let you go."

"But Mom —"

"No buts, Kirby. E Street is just too far away," his father admonished. "What if something had happened to you? If you'd gotten hurt? I'm guessing roller hockey is a very physical sport, with lots of bodychecking and cheap shots. Or what if you'd gotten lost? You could have been skating around for hours, after dark, trying to figure out where you were."

"We don't know anything about those kids or their parents, either. I'm sure you'll find some other friends to play with tomorrow, closer to home," his mother added in her patient, therapist voice.

Kirby couldn't believe his ears. "I don't want to find other friends!" he yelled. "I want these friends!"

Ignoring his parents' shocked faces, he stormed out of the kitchen. He hated it when his parents treated him like a baby. Kicking a pebble as far as he could, he trudged into the garage and started rummaging through boxes of stuff. He pulled out an old deflated basketball, a skateboard with a wheel missing, and a pair of muddy soccer cleats.

As he did, he remembered when his mother had packed the gear up. She had commented wryly that he was pretty hard on sports equipment, then asked him if he still wanted it all or if they could get rid of it before the move.

"Don't throw it out!" he had insisted. "I might use it again someday."

His mother had given him a disbelieving look and mumbled something about his trying out sports like he was trying on new clothes: If he didn't like them after a few months, he just tossed them aside. But she had packed up the gear anyway.

Now Kirby fished around, looking for his old hockey stuff. After a minute of searching, he found it and tried putting it on. It was all too tight on him.

Well, thought Kirby, at least that means I'm getting bigger.

On the other hand, it also meant that if he was able to convince his parents to let him play, there was no way he could use the equipment. Worse than being too small, his old stuff was for playing goalie. He didn't want to play goalie anymore. In ice hockey, he'd never liked standing there in goal while everybody else was skating around. Especially since he'd always been faster on skates than any of his friends. And another thing he hated about playing goalie — the worst part — was being shot at.

Besides, he wasn't about to make an enemy of Lainie by competing for her spot.

Kirby started to take the gear off but then had an idea. Maybe if his parents saw how small it was on him, they'd realize that he wasn't a little kid anymore. He waddled back inside, in full regalia.

His mother took one look at him and smiled ruefully. "Oh, my!" she said. "That outfit doesn't fit you anymore, does it?"

"Well, it *is* two years old. I've grown up a lot since you bought it." He started to take the equipment off, then glanced up at his parents. "I'm sorry I yelled before. But listen, I didn't get lost today, did I? I used the map." He pulled it from his back pocket to prove his point.

"Plus, their goalie lives close to here, so I can always come most of the way home with her, like I did today." Of course, G Street was only two blocks closer than E Street, but he decided not to mention that.

"And all the kids I met today were really nice," he added. Not counting, of course, the two boys he had run into on Bates Avenue. But after all, they didn't count. He wasn't going to be playing hockey with them, was he?

His father heaved a sigh.

"All that may be true, but as you're so clearly demonstrating, you don't have the proper equipment even if we did agree to let you play. And given how your interest in a particular sport usually fades after a short time, I'm not sure your mother and I are ready to lay down money on expensive new equipment for you."

Thinking back to the stuff he had just unearthed in the garage, Kirby knew better than to protest. So he took a different tactic instead.

"What if I work around the house to help pay you back for new equipment?" he asked.

His father shook his head. "Even if you save your allowance, it's not just money that's the problem. Beyond everything else we've mentioned, we're against the idea of you playing in the street. If you want to skate, there are plenty of sidewalks right here in our neighborhood. But playing hockey in the street just sounds dangerous."

"What?" Taken by surprise, Kirby looked from his mom to his dad and back again. "You used to let me skate in the street back in Minford. Just so long as I was careful, you said it was okay. And no more than two or three cars came down E Street the whole time I was there!"

There was a short silence. Then his mom said to his father, "Well, he's got a point there. But that doesn't mean we're in favor of you playing," she added quickly as Kirby's face brightened. "We just don't know enough about this town, its streets, or your new friends yet. I'm sorry, Kirby, but until we do, I want you to stick around here."

"I'm telling you, it's not dangerous!" Kirby insisted. But he could tell his words were falling on deaf ears. After all, what did he know? He was just their son.

If only someone else could talk to them, and make them see reason. If only he could call one of the kids from E Street.

Unfortunately he didn't remember any of their last names. Lainie had told him hers, but he couldn't remember it, except that it was also the name of somebody famous.

And then there was that Marty kid. . . . Lainie had called him by his last name once. What was it . . . ?

"Bledsoe!" Kirby shouted out loud, remembering. He went over to the kitchen phone, dialed Information, and asked for Bledsoe. Sure enough, there was one — a Kenneth and Ilene Bledsoe, on Ridley Lane. Kirby wrote down the number and dialed it.

"Hello?"

"Hi, is Marty there?"

"Speaking. Who's this?"

"This is Kirby. Remember me from today? The short kid?"

"Oh, yeah. Did I give you my number?"

"I got it from Information. Listen, could you do me a favor? I'm trying to convince my parents to let me play hockey with you guys. But they're freaking out. They've already said I can't come to your practice tomorrow. They say it's too dangerous, that E Street is too busy, and the new equipment is too expensive."

"They don't know what they're talking about, okay? First of all, in roller hockey, you're not allowed to check with the body. Anybody makes heavy contact, it's a penalty, understand? So it's not even really a contact sport. And because you wear padding, you don't have to worry about getting hit with the puck or a stick. Worst you can do is fall on your rear and stuff like that. As for expensive, you can get used gear pretty cheap."

37

"You can?" Kirby felt his heart pounding. Things were definitely looking up. "Listen, can you tell this all to my parents?"

"Sure, but they won't believe me. I'm just a kid. Hold on, and I'll put my parents on with them."

"Fantastic!" Kirby turned to his parents, who had been watching the whole time. "Mom! Dad! Pick up the phone. Somebody wants to talk to you."

His dad went into the living room to grab the cordless extension, and his mom took the phone from Kirby. Five minutes later, after a real gab-fest, Kirby's parents hung up.

"Well, what do you know?" Kirby's dad said as he came back into the kitchen. "Looks like we've got our first dinner invitation here in Valemont — all thanks to you, son!"

Kirby smiled and said a quiet "Yes!" under his breath. Maybe the Bledsoes would talk his parents into letting him play!

4

The next morning, Kirby busied himself unpacking his things and setting up his new room. It was definitely bigger than his old room, which had basically been the attic, dressed up to look like a small bedroom. But Kirby had liked the way the ceiling slanted low over the top of the bed. Every once in a while, after reading to him, his dad would bump his head on the wall with a big thud. It was never as bad as it sounded, but it always made Kirby giggle to see his dad look so silly — and his dad had always laughed, too. Kirby was going to miss his old room.

Still, this one had a lot to recommend it. There was a big double closet, instead of the tiny one with the low door, into which he'd had to cram every last thing in the world he wasn't using. Here, he'd actually be able to get organized.

He started looking through the posters that used to hang on the walls of his old room, to see which ones he wanted to put up now. Funny, but they didn't look as cool to him as they used to. He was getting too old for the animal ones, and the movie ones were of old, old movies — at least two years old!

One of the sports ones was of Mario Lemieux. He'd since retired from hockey, but for some reason, Kirby really wanted to hang up that poster of him. Maybe it was because of what had happened on E Street the day before. At any rate, he taped it up right next to where his head would be when he lay down to sleep. It would be the last thing he would see tonight — and every night — before he turned out the light. Cool.

Tonight. They'd be going over to the Bledsoes for dinner tonight. Kirby could hardly wait. He hoped Marty would want to be friends, apart from skating. Kirby missed his old friends. He wondered what Evan and Rachel and Devon were up to. Probably ice-skating to keep cool.

After lunch, Kirby finished putting his room together, then helped his mom move some light pieces of furniture around to different spots to see how they looked. By the time they were finished, it was three-thirty.

His thoughts turned to the E Street Skates. They'd be expecting him to play in half an hour. Would Marty bother to explain why he wasn't going to show up? Maybe Marty had already told the others about his parents. They'd probably think his folks were weird.

No, he decided. They would think *he* was weird for not standing up to his parents more. They'd think he was a total wimp.

Am I a wimp? he wondered. Kirby thought about it for a minute, then decided he wasn't. It wasn't like he was afraid to play or anything. He just wasn't the kind of kid who'd go against his parents' orders. If the kids didn't like him because of that, too bad.

Anyhow, after tonight, it wouldn't be a problem. Marty and his parents would surely be able to convince his parents that playing in-line hockey in the street was safe.

Yeah. He could hardly wait for dinner at the Bledsoes. He was feeling hungry already.

"No, no, no!" Mr. Bledsoe let out a big belly laugh and slapped Kirby's dad warmly on the knee. "Dangerous? My goodness, the kids barely touch each other!"

"They're not allowed to check each other at all," Mrs. Bledsoe added. She was a tall, pretty woman who looked like an athlete, with dark brown hair, suntanned skin, and a bright smile. Marty's dad was huge in every way — tall, with a big belly and a shock of dark hair that kept falling down his forehead. He was a lawyer, and Kirby thought he must be a good one, because he sure seemed to be convincing the jury tonight.

In fact, the four grown-ups seemed to be getting along great. Now, just when Kirby was about to explode with impatience, the subject of hockey had finally come up.

"You know, the equipment can get pretty expensive," Kirby's dad was saying. "We spent quite a bit on a goalie outfit for Kirby a couple years ago, and he's already grown out of it."

Mrs. Bledsoe came to the rescue. "Well, we know!" she agreed. "It's outrageous how much sports equipment can cost if you let it get out of hand. That's why the parents in Valemont set up a used sports gear exchange!"

"Oh, that sounds just fantastic!" Kirby's mom said, brightening.

"Yes," Mrs. Bledsoe went on, "in fact, we're having the next one Saturday morning at the middle school. You'll be able to pick up anything you need there — just bring along that old goalie outfit and whatever else you might not need anymore."

"Well, then, that's one problem solved," Kirby's dad said. "Now, what about the traffic?"

"I'll be honest with you, Phil," Mr. Bledsoe

replied, leaning forward. "There *are* occasional cars, but the kids are real careful. And the times I've been there, there's never been any traffic to speak of. It's almost like playing on a dead end."

"So you've watched them play a good bit?" Kirby's dad asked.

"Yeah, it's wonderful," Mr. Bledsoe replied. "We've never had any problem with Marty skating there. Now, I can understand your concern, but you have nothing to worry about. You'll like the kids — they're a nice bunch, and we parents all get along, too. When they have a game, a lot of us show up to cheer them on. Once in a while we have a team family barbecue. It's a real social thing."

"Well, that's good," Kirby's mom said. Kirby knew she was looking to make friends of her own here in Valemont. "And you're sure about the traffic, and the violence of the game."

"Oh, yes, Mary," Marty's mom said, putting a hand on her arm. "You needn't worry. I know there are some kids out there who watch the professional ice hockey games on TV and think they can start banging the other kids with their bodies and sticks in roller hockey, too. But it isn't like that on E Street."

"What about the teams they play against?" Kirby's mom asked.

There was a silence that went on a little too long. Kirby saw that Marty was biting his lip.

"Well," Marty's dad spoke up, "the Bates Avenue team has some older kids on it — one's even fifteen, I think. And a couple of them can get a little rough. But none of the kids has ever gotten seriously hurt."

Kirby thought that would make his parents feel better about it. But looking at them, he saw them exchange a worried glance.

Mr. Bledsoe spoke up. "Marty, why don't you take Kirby up and show him your room, okay?"

Marty took the hint, and he and Kirby headed upstairs. But when they reached the landing,

Kirby stopped Marty, putting a finger to his lips. Marty understood, and they sat on the stairs to listen.

Marty's dad was still talking. "Look, Phil, Mary, let me be frank with you. I don't think you're doing the boy any favors by forbidding him to play. Stop me if you think I'm out of bounds here, but why don't you at least give him a chance? It might be the best thing that ever happened to him."

"I know he wants very much to be a part of it," Kirby's mom said. "And I do want him to make friends here. But you know, Kirby's not a big boy, he's small and thin, and I dread the thought of him getting knocked around by some rough fifteen-year-old."

"I understand, Mary," Marty's dad assured her. "Look, you two have got to make your own decisions. I just couldn't let the chance go by without speaking my piece. Would you like some dessert, by the way?"

After that, they didn't talk about hockey for a few minutes. Kirby could tell that Mr. Bledsoe wanted to give the jury — er, his parents — time to think things over.

"Want to see my room?" Marty whispered.

"Sure," Kirby said. "Might as well. Sitting here isn't going to help."

Marty's room was incredible. There were signed baseball bats and balls hanging from the walls, and shelves lined with trophies for every sport you could think of. Obviously Marty was an all-around athlete.

Marty seemed like a nice kid, too. Not stuck up or anything. Kirby liked him, especially since he and his parents were helping convince Kirby's mom and dad. He was dying to ask him about that afternoon's practice, and what the other kids had said when he didn't show up, but he didn't. He wasn't sure he wanted to know.

"Let's go back down and see what they say," Kirby said, unable to stand the suspense any longer.

"Okay," Marty said. "Come on."

They went back downstairs, and two slices of

chocolate cake were waiting for them at the table. All the parents were smiling. A good sign, Kirby thought.

"Kirby," his dad said, "your mother and I have given it some thought. Mr. and Mrs. Bledsoe have been making some good points, and we feel we ought to give this street hockey thing a chance. So we'll go to the used gear exchange on Saturday morning and get you what you need. And then you can go to the Saturday practice — your mother and I will hang around and watch. Okay?"

"You mean I can play?" Kirby gasped. It was almost too good to be true.

"One step at a time," his mother said. "We'll see. For now, let's watch you practice once."

"Yes!" Kirby said, pumping his fist in the air and slapping Marty with a high five. "All right! Thanks, Mom and Dad — you're the best!"

–

5

It was raining on Friday when Kirby woke up. Thunder rumbled in the distance. Kirby looked at his alarm clock and wondered why it was ringing — he hadn't set it. Then he realized that it was the telephone by his bed. He picked up the receiver.

It was Marty, inviting him to go with him and two of the other E Street Skates to the movies at the mall that afternoon. A comedy about hockey was playing.

"It starts at two o'clock. Can you make it?"

Kirby said, "Can you pick me up?"

"Sure, my mom's taking everyone in the van. See you at one-thirty?"

"Sure!" Kirby hung up, and only then realized

that he hadn't checked with his mom first.

Luckily it was fine with her. That afternoon, when the van pulled up, she gave him a hug and some money and said, "Have a great time, Kirby. I'm so glad you're making so many new friends."

Kirby was happy, too, but he didn't want to get all mushy about it. They weren't really his friends yet, and if his mom and dad didn't like what they saw tomorrow at practice, they might never be.

"Bye, Mom," he simply said. He gave her a peck on the cheek, then ran outside and through the rain to the van.

Everyone greeted him by shaking his hand, thumbs-locking style, and telling him their names again.

Trevor McDonough was the team's other forward. He had sand-colored hair and looked right at Kirby when he shook hands. Kirby remembered him as number 7. He was smaller than Marty but a good skater and shooter — also an intense competitor. Kirby recalled Trevor shouting about how his shot was a goal.

Then there was Nick, the overweight one. He had dark hair in a buzz cut and a round, red face. His hand felt cold and clammy, but Kirby liked the way he smiled and laughed.

Jamal was almost as small and thin as Kirby. But whereas Kirby was blond and pale with glasses, Jamal had dark brown skin, curly black hair, brown eyes, and no glasses. Kirby remembered he wasn't much of a skater. But when he shook Kirby's hand, he really shook it.

"Glad to meet you!" he said with a big smile. "Now I'm not the smallest kid on the team!"

Kirby laughed and settled back for the ride to the theater. That's when he realized that someone was missing.

"Where's Lainie?" he asked.

"Lainie?" Marty repeated. "Probably with her friends or something. Why?"

"You mean, she's not one of *your* friends?"

"Yeah, I guess."

"We just don't generally hang out with her," Trevor explained.

"Well . . . why not?" Kirby persisted.

There was a sudden, uncomfortable silence in the van. Kirby looked up front at Mrs. Bledsoe, who was driving. She was staying totally out of the conversation.

"What, do you like her or something?" Trevor asked.

"No!" Kirby responded automatically. "I mean, yeah, of course I like her — don't you like her?"

He felt himself going red as Jamal and Nick laughed. "Aw, forget it," Marty said, clapping him on the shoulder. "We're just ragging you. We do that with each other all the time."

Kirby sat back, relieved. "Well, maybe she'd like to come with us," he said.

Marty turned to his mother. "Mom, can we drive by Lainie's and see if she can come?"

"Sure thing," his mom said. "And I think that's a very nice idea, too."

Five minutes later, Lainie hopped into the van, excited. "Thanks for inviting me!" she said.

"Thank Kirby," Trevor said. "It was his idea."

"Oh. Well, thanks, then," she said, giving Kirby a big smile. "I take it the rest of you approved?"

Everyone laughed together. This was going to be a fun afternoon, Kirby decided.

The movie turned out not to be so great, but at least it had been good for a few laughs. The funniest things were the comments the kids whispered to each other.

The next morning, as promised, Kirby's mom and dad took him to the gear exchange. It was a bigger event than he'd thought it would be. There were people from a lot of the nearby towns, and even one family from Minford!

Kirby knew the kid, but not really well. He was two years younger than Kirby. Still, he was so excited to see someone from Minford that he went over and nearly hugged the kid.

"Noel! It's me! Kirby!"

Noel gave him a weird look. "Oh, yeah . . . I remember you. You moved, right?"

"Yeah. I live here now."

"Oh." Noel moved off, uninterested, and began to look at old uniforms. Embarrassed, Kirby rejoined his parents.

"Let's get this over with, okay?" he said. "I want to get to E Street."

They handed in Kirby's old goalie outfit and the other useless gear from the garage and were given vouchers for its value. Then they went to the section that had stuff in Kirby's size and picked out the best gear they could find: a pair of hockey gloves, shin guards, padded hockey pants, and shoulder pads. Kirby already had elbow pads and wrist guards. His regular skates would have to do for now.

Helmets were not part of the exchange. "Once helmets have taken a pounding, they don't absorb shocks as well," the man in charge told them. "So we don't trade them. Best to get a new one at the sporting goods store."

So Reilly's Sporting Goods was their next stop. Kirby got a white helmet, matching the ones Marty and the others had. His parents also got him a new stick and some black tape to tape it up with.

"Can I get a uniform, too?" he begged. "Those over there are the same ones the other kids have."

"The white ones with the red numbers?" his dad asked.

"Yes. Please, Dad? Mom? I'll help pay with my allowance money." He pulled a few bills from his pocket and held them out.

His dad and mom looked at each other wearily and smiled. "All right, Kirby," his mom said. "But remember, it doesn't mean we're letting you join the team. We'll have to wait and see about that."

Kirby nodded quickly, but he didn't really pay much attention to the warning his mom had given. After all, he thought, why wouldn't they let me join the team? They've already gotten me the equipment and the uniform!

They paid the cashier and drove from downtown to E Street. "Turn here," Kirby told his mother, who was driving. "And park before you get to the net."

55

They pulled over, and Kirby got out. He already had his skates and gear on. All the way there, he'd been getting suited up in the backseat. The other kids let out a whoop when they saw him.

"He's here!" Jamal· yelled. "It's Wayne Gretzky!"

Kirby laughed, realizing that his parents had bought him number 99. "I guess I'd better be good!" he joked.

There weren't any other parents around, Kirby noticed. His own had gotten out of the car and were watching them. It made Kirby suddenly uncomfortable. What will the other kids think? he wondered.

None of them seemed to notice, though. They were too busy passing the puck around and shooting it at Lainie. Trevor passed the puck to Kirby and said, "Go for it, hotshot!"

Kirby took the pass and skated toward the blue chalk line the kids had drawn across the street. He wound up for a slap shot.

"Car!" Lainie yelled just as Kirby was about to fire the puck. She grabbed the net and pulled it toward the side of the street. The car went roaring by. The driver had barely slowed down.

"Can you believe that guy?" Nick said. "Jerk!" he called after the speeding car.

"Come on, let's get back to work," Marty said. He helped Lainie return the net to its chalk mark in the middle of the street, then skated off to play defense. "Take another shot, Kirby. Kirby?"

Kirby was watching his parents. They were deep in conversation. Uh-oh, Kirby thought. He hoped they hadn't gotten the wrong idea, seeing that car speed by.

He took the puck off Trevor's stick again and tried to skate by Marty with it. Marty stayed close, trying to knock it away. Kirby kept his body between Marty and the puck.

Getting an idea, Kirby suddenly fed the puck between Marty's legs and, with a quick spin, picked it up on the other side of him.

Marty was taken totally by surprise. He spun

around backward, tripped over his own stick, and fell right on top of Kirby. Both of them crashed onto the pavement. Neither boy was hurt, thanks to their protective gear. But Kirby knew his parents had been watching while a kid twice his size had fallen right on top of him.

"Car!" Lainie called out again. E Street was a one-way street, so Lainie, always facing the traffic, was the first to spot oncoming cars. Once again, she pulled the net away, and the others skated to the curb.

Now a procession of cars came barreling down the block. No sooner did Lainie and Marty replace the net than another group of cars forced them to the side again.

"How come there are so many cars?" Kirby asked Marty anxiously.

"It's bad on weekends in summer," Marty explained. "A lot of cars cut through here on their way to Longwood Lake."

"Oh. Couldn't your dad have mentioned that

the other night? My parents are getting upset. Look at them."

"They don't look too happy," Marty agreed. "Come on, let's just play. Once they see you score a goal, they'll loosen up. Lainie — let Kirby score one, okay?"

Lainie frowned. Clearly she didn't like the idea of making herself look bad. "Okay," she said with a shrug. "But just this once."

The traffic finally let up. Once more, Kirby took the pass at center ice from Trevor. Marty purposely let him get free for the shot, and Kirby wound up for the big blast.

His stick hit the puck with a resounding *thwack*. The puck sailed toward Lainie, who ducked in real fear. But the shot was just a bit high. It flew just over the net, and kept going — right smack into the windshield of Kirby's parents' car!

"Aaaaaagh!" Kirby screamed. "No! No! I didn't do that! It was an accident — Mom! Dad! Wait!"

His mom and dad were already at the car, looking at the shattered windshield. "It was an accident!" Kirby repeated as he skated up to them.

"Well, we'll have to get it fixed," his father said, tight-lipped. "Right now. And you'll have to come with us, Kirby."

"But —"

"No buts," his mom said. "We'll discuss it in the car."

Kirby said a sad good-bye to his friends, then got in, and they drove off.

"It's not just the windshield, Kirby," his mother said as Kirby fought back tears in the backseat. "It's all the traffic, with those crazy drivers . . ."

His father agreed. "It's dangerous, playing in the street. You'll have to do other things with your new friends. Playing hockey in the street is out."

Kirby felt tears tumbling down his cheeks. Great. There went his only friends. His whole life was ruined! What was he going to do now?

6

For the rest of that day, Kirby barricaded himself in his room and didn't come out except to use the bathroom or sneak some snacks. He played a lot of video games and watched a lot of TV. He didn't say a word to either of his parents — not even when his mom knocked on the door at ten o'clock to tell him to shut off the lights and go to sleep.

The next morning, he felt awful. He hadn't slept very well. On top of feeling crummy about not playing hockey, he felt guilty about not talking to his parents — especially after breaking their windshield. He decided he couldn't take it anymore.

His mom and dad were down in the kitchen, eating muffins. "Hi," he said softly, taking his regular seat at the table. "I'm sorry about everything. I didn't mean to break the windshield, and I guess I should have said good night to you."

"Oh, honey," his mother said, getting up to give him a hug. "We're sorry, too."

"I shouldn't have dragged you away from there just like that," his dad said. "I guess I overreacted."

"So . . . I can play?" Kirby dared to ask.

"Well, no. Not in the street," his mother said. "There are just too many cars, and they drive too fast."

"But it wasn't like that the other time!" Kirby protested. "Marty says it's just on the summer weekends, 'cause people go to the lake."

"I'm sure there's some truth in that," his father said, "but unless you can find some other place to play, it's no deal. Your safety comes first."

Kirby sighed, realizing there was no use talking about it any further. He knew his parents. When they said no like that, they never changed their minds.

He knew they were right about his safety, too. But why couldn't they understand how important this was to him?

Looking for sympathy, he went into the living room and called Marty on the phone.

"Man, that really bites," Marty said when Kirby filled him in on the latest. "None of us could believe you cracked your parents' windshield."

"Me neither."

"That was some shot," Marty said. "We could have used you on the team. Well, maybe they'll change their minds."

"Not my parents. You don't know them." Kirby sighed loudly.

"Well, if they do, we're practicing again on Wednesday at four o'clock. And there's a game on Saturday at noon."

"A game?" Kirby's heart sank. A real game — and he wouldn't get to be in it!

The days seemed to drag on. Kirby's uncle and aunt brought his bike with them when they visited from Minford on Sunday, so he rode a little. He fixed up his room to look as much like Marty's as possible — which was hard, because he didn't have nearly as many trophies or sports posters.

He tried reading a book but couldn't get into it. His mind kept wandering back to thoughts of playing hockey.

He played too many video games and watched too many stupid shows on TV. He helped his mother cook a meal, which was totally boring, even though he usually enjoyed cooking. His dad challenged him to a chess game, and Kirby let him win.

When Wednesday afternoon rolled around, Kirby was going crazy with boredom. He decided to risk going against his parents' wishes — at least a little bit — and sneak over to E Street. But he'd ride his bike, not skate. His parents hadn't forbidden him to do that, he reasoned. He ignored the little voice inside his head that scolded him for his disobedience. It would be painful enough having to sit and watch the practice without playing, but anything was better than hanging around home alone.

This time, as he passed Bates Avenue, he looked left and right. Sure enough, there was a net set up down the block. The Bad Boys were practicing for their game with the Skates. On an impulse, Kirby rode toward them.

"Out of the way!" one of them shouted as he passed by. "Move!"

"Hey, it's that geeky kid!" said another. Kirby recognized Buzz Cut from in front of the grocery store. "Yo, geek! What's your name?"

"Kirby," said Kirby. "What's yours?"

The boy sneered. "Killer. And this is my buddy

Spike," he said, indicating the kid with the mirror sunglasses under his hockey helmet. "Wanna do something about it?"

"Uh . . . no," Kirby said.

"So get lost," Killer said.

"Yeah. Get a life," Spike agreed. "Beat it, before we use you for a hockey puck!"

That got the whole team laughing. Boy, Kirby thought as he pedaled away, no wonder they call themselves the Bad Boys. It's the perfect name for them.

Kirby headed straight for E Street, where his friends were in the middle of a pass-and-shoot drill.

"Hey, Kirby!" Nick called out when he saw him. "Did your parents decide to let you play?"

"Duh," Trevor said. "He's on his bike. Does it look like he came to play?"

"I'm just here to watch," Kirby said. "Go ahead."

He sat on the curb opposite the net. From here, he could talk to Lainie while she stood in the net.

"I can't believe what bad luck you had Saturday," she said. "Those jerks speeding down the street like that — and then you breaking the windshield!"

"I know," Kirby agreed. "My parents said it was playing in the street that bothered them, though, not the windshield."

"Funny how there aren't any cars around today at all, huh?" Lainie said.

"Yeah. Anyway, if you guys ever play someplace that isn't in the street, let me know. Maybe I can play with you then."

Just then, a shot came at Lainie. She reached out and deflected it with her blocker. "Time out!" she called out, taking off her mask. "What did you just say?" she asked, turning to Kirby.

"I said, I bet my parents would let me play, if only it wasn't in traffic."

"Well, hey, that's what I thought you said! You know, when we play Bates Avenue, we don't play here."

"Yeah," Kirby said, "but I don't think they'd let

me play on Bates Avenue either. There's more traffic there than here."

"No, we don't play there — we play in this old overgrown parking lot down by the railroad tracks."

"In a parking lot?" Kirby repeated. "The owners let you do that?"

"It used to be part of the factory next door, but the owners went out of business, so now the town owns it. Nobody uses the lot except us. It's empty. There's nothing over there — and no traffic at all."

"You're kidding me." A ray of light was beginning to dawn in Kirby's mind.

"No, seriously. There are weeds and stuff growing out of the pavement. It's a real dump. But there aren't any cars."

"Then how come you guys don't practice there, too?" Kirby asked.

"The pavement's not that great," Lainie said with a shrug. "It's got lots of cracks and bumps and stuff. It's better here, cars or no cars. Only we can't have a game here, because we'd have to keep stopping play all the time."

"Right. Well, maybe my parents will let me play in the game on Saturday since it's not on the street!"

Marty heard this last part as he skated up to them. "You can play Saturday? I thought your folks wouldn't let you."

Kirby explained, and soon all the team members had gathered around and were making plans.

"How can he play with us if he can't practice?" Trevor wanted to know. "Just asking. I mean, we've got plays and everything."

"That's true," Marty said. "But he could learn them. I can go over to his house and work on the plays with him."

"I'm a fast learner," Kirby assured them.

"But then we'll have six players," Jamal said, a little nervously.

"Don't worry, Jamal — nobody's going to take your place," Marty said. "Kirby here can come off the bench as a substitute when one of us gets tired."

"Or when one of us gets a stick in the guts," Trevor said. "You know how those guys play."

"I saw them on the way over here," Kirby said. "They're pretty mean, aren't they?"

"Them? Mean?" Lainie said sarcastically. "Hey, that's why it's going to feel so great to beat them. And you're going to help us, Kirby."

"If I can just talk my parents into it, I'll be there!" Kirby said excitedly. "See you!" And with that, he got on his bike and pedaled like mad for home.

7

Hey, Mom, Dad, guess what?" Kirby sure hoped his mom and dad were going to go for this plan.

"Well, you certainly look excited, whatever it is," his mom said, setting Kirby a place at the dinner table.

He sat right down and looked from his dad to his mom. "The E Street Skates are going to let me be on the team for their game on Saturday — even though I can't come for practice!"

Kirby's dad frowned. "Kirby, I thought we explained to you about playing in the str —"

"But it isn't in the street, Dad!" Kirby interrupted. "It's in an abandoned parking lot by the railroad tracks!"

"Oh. I see." His dad settled back in his chair

and looked thoughtful. "Mary? What do you think?"

"Let me give Ilene Bledsoe a call," she said. Five minutes later she returned. "Well, Ilene says there hasn't been a problem with the kids playing there, so it sounds all right to me. It would be nice to see all that equipment we got you put to use. But I want to be there to cheer you on, Kirby — just in case."

Kirby held his breath, then let it out with a whoosh when his father nodded in agreement.

"Thanks, Mom! Thank you, Dad! I can't believe I'm really going to play!" Kirby hugged them both, then started pacing the dining room floor. "I'm only a sub, of course, but I know they're going to play me, just 'cause they want to see if I can skate and stuff."

"Sit down and eat your dinner, honey," his mom said. "You're going to need to build up your strength."

"Oh. Yeah. Right," Kirby said distractedly. He

sat down and ate, thinking only of the big game.

He could see it now. He would have the puck, and that big kid from Bates Avenue, Spike, would come barreling toward him, elbows out. Kirby would duck at the last minute, and the guy would go flying! Kirby wouldn't even look back until he'd smashed a goal past that other kid — the one who'd called him a geek. Yeah. That's what he was going to do. He was going to make them pay. . . .

"Kirby?" His dad was tapping him on the arm.

"Score!" Kirby shouted. "I mean — what, Dad?"

"Eat your dinner, son," his dad said. "You can dream after you go to bed, okay?"

Kirby decided that his dad was right. What he needed to do with his waking time, between now and Saturday, was to practice. He wanted to make himself ready for the big game in every possible way.

The next day, Marty came over and spent

almost the whole day. First he helped Kirby tape up his stick properly, so it wouldn't crack and so Kirby would be able to handle the puck better.

When they were done, they went out and practiced in Kirby's driveway, where it widened out for the basketball court. Marty showed Kirby some cool moves with and without the puck, including one where he turned 360 degrees around the defender, picking the puck up again on the other side.

"Where'd you learn all those moves?" Kirby wanted to know.

"From a videotape."

"Do you still have it?"

"Are you kidding?" Marty laughed. "I brought it with me."

"All right! Man, I hope I get to play on Saturday."

"You'll play," Marty said. "I'm the captain, remember?" He grinned and clapped Kirby on the shoulder pad.

Just then, a car horn sounded behind them. "There's my mom. I've got to go to practice," Marty said.

Kirby sighed. "Say hi for me. Tell them I'll see them at the game."

Marty nodded and skated to the curb. "Keep practicing!" he called out before getting in. "Because you're going to play!"

By the time Saturday morning arrived, Kirby had watched the video ten or twelve times. He felt like he was as ready as he'd ever be. But he was so nervous, he didn't talk much to his parents over breakfast, and thankfully they didn't try to make him talk.

Around eleven, they all piled into the old station wagon and headed for the industrial area down by the tracks, just the other side of downtown. "That's Bates Avenue," Kirby told his parents as they passed it.

"Is that the team you're playing?" his mom asked.

"Yeah. The Bates Avenue Bad Boys," Kirby said.

"Whew. Sounds menacing," his dad remarked.

"Oh, come on, honey, it's just a name," his mom said with a laugh.

Kirby tried to laugh, too. The last thing he wanted was for his parents to worry about his safety. But the truth was, Kirby himself was starting to feel distinctly scared.

He knew that it was against the rules of in-line roller hockey to bodycheck. But he also guessed that if any team was likely to cheat, it was the Bates Avenue Bad Boys. And who better for them to pick on than the little kid they thought was a geek?

Kirby's mom pulled the car over beside the parking lot. The lot had a rusty, six-foot-high chain-link fence all around it, to keep people from parking their cars there. Kirby figured it was because the town wanted to make money from the parking meters and didn't want to let people park for free.

Inside, someone had sketched out a rink with chalk. The chalk oval was about 180 feet long and 80 feet wide, and the chain-link fence bordered it on two sides. On the other sides, plastic curbs had been laid out. There was a blue line across the center, and a pair of two-foot-wide faceoff circles had been drawn in either zone. There was also a faceoff circle in the middle of the rink.

Kirby was surprised at how many weeds were growing out of the cracked pavement. They ought to at least make it look nice, he thought. No wonder no one had bought the property. Of course, the boarded-up factory next door didn't help either. Oh, well. At least someone had swept away whatever broken glass had been there.

The Bates Avenue Bad Boys were skating around, slapping shots at their goalie and slamming each other into the fence just for fun. Some of their parents were standing on the sidelines, talking to each other and totally ignoring their kids. Kirby shook his head, picturing his mom throwing a fit if he ever fooled around like that on skates.

"Are those the boys you're playing against?" his mother asked anxiously.

"Yup," Kirby answered. "Don't worry, Mom — they're just trying to look tough to psych us out."

"Well, I hope you're not all going to go out there and do the same!" she said in a huff.

Kirby just laughed, and skated over to where the E Street Skates were huddled. All of his pals shouted a greeting and clapped him on the back.

"Boy, are we glad to see you!" Nick said. "Those guys seem to get bigger every time we play them."

"Don't worry about them," Trevor said. "Marty and I can skate rings around them!"

"Not if they deck you," Nick shot back.

"If they shoot past me, I'm ducking," Jamal said. "I'm not going to block it. They shoot too hard."

"Don't worry about it, they're not going to score off me," Lainie said. "I hate those guys. They're always giving me a hard time because I'm a girl playing with the boys."

Just then, one of the Bad Boys skated up to them. "Just want you to know, you guys are lucky," he said, staring straight at Marty. "We would have laid you flat on your backs if there weren't so many parents here watching. Next time, you'd better watch out. Pump some iron, wimps." He skated off again.

"Jerk," Trevor said under his breath. "I should have busted him one."

"Why, so you could be more like him?" Marty asked sarcastically. "I don't think so. Why be stupid?"

"Really," Nick agreed. "The caveman days are over."

"C'mon," Lainie said. "It's time to meet and beat the competition."

As they skated over to the Bad Boys, Kirby glanced back at where he'd left his parents.

They were standing with the Bledsoes, who were introducing them to the other parents. Some had brought folding chairs to sit on as they watched the action — from a safe distance, of course, since a flying puck can be dangerous and spectators don't wear protective gear.

The Bad Boys, in their black uniforms with silver numbers, gathered together while Marty went over the rules of play.

"Out of bounds is a frozen puck," he said. "We'll have two twenty-two-minute halves, and the clock never stops. Five minutes between halves. No checking with the stick or the body, understood? Okay. Now for the coin toss. Who's got a coin?"

Jamal pulled a quarter from his pocket. Killer stepped forward to represent the Bad Boys. Marty reached to shake Killer's outstretched hand, but at the last minute, Killer jerked his hand back, sneering. Marty dropped his hand but didn't say anything.

"Okay, call it in the air." Jamal flipped the coin.

"Tails!" Marty said. The coin dropped to the ground.

"Yes, tails it is," Jamal said. "Which goal are we going to defend?"

This, it turned out, was an important choice. The lot sloped slightly downhill, and there were more cracks near the downhill goal. Marty pointed uphill. "We'll take that one."

"Figures. Let's play," Killer growled as he skated off to his position.

All the parents started cheering their kids as the teams lined up for the opening faceoff. Kirby skated off to the sideline. Across from him, four Bad Boy subs waited to enter the game. At least I'm not the only one, thought Kirby.

One of the Bad Boy subs dropped the puck, and the game was on. Marty won the faceoff and got the puck to Trevor, who quickly skated toward the Bad Boys' goal. Marty followed him in, but the defense was all over them, grappling for the puck, which soon came loose. Spike got it on his stick, and passed it across the blue line to Killer.

Right away, Kirby could tell that the Skates were in trouble. Nick had come too far forward on defense, skating himself right out of the play. Now poor Jamal was all that was left between the Bad Boys and Lainie. Killer made a move as though he was going to shove Jamal, and Jamal, terrified, ducked. Killer easily skated past him, while Spike went straight for the goal mouth.

Killer moved in close, faked, then flicked a wrist shot above Lainie's left shoulder. Somehow, incredibly, she blocked the shot. But the rebound skittered right onto Spike's stick!

He shoved it clumsily at the goal. Lainie fell on it. Both Bad Boys hacked at her glove, trying to dislodge it, and before she or her teammates could think to call the puck dead, one of the Bad Boys had jammed it into the goal.

A shout went up from the parents on the E Street side of the rink. "Come on, guys!" Mr. Bledsoe called. "That puck was dead!"

The Bad Boys paid no attention. They mobbed each other, cheering. One to nothing already, and the game has barely started, Kirby thought.

After that, the Skates seemed to dig in. Trevor and Marty put some pressure on the offensive end, getting off one or two good shots whenever they could free themselves from the Bad Boys' smothering defense.

But the main reason the score remained 1–0 was because every time the puck came into the Skates' end, Nick and Jamal just slammed it right back down the rink instead of manuevering for a good pass. There were a lot of icing calls against the Skates, and that meant a lot of faceoffs in their own end. Luckily Lainie managed to hold off the barrage.

That is, until Trevor tripped over some bad cracks in the pavement, and Killer and Spike mounted another two-on-one rush, with Nick again too far forward.

This time, when Jamal ducked, his stick caught Spike's shot and deflected it past Lainie into the goal. Lainie shrieked in frustration and pounded her stick on the pavement. "Come on, defense!" she yelled at Jamal and Nick.

"Hey, go easy!" Marty told her. "They're doing the best they can."

Lainie looked over at Kirby and then at Marty. Marty knew what she meant. "Yeah, okay, take a break, Nick."

"Me?" Nick seemed stunned. "I'm not tired."

"I'm tired!" Jamal said, getting to his feet clumsily and skating off the rink.

"Let's go, let's go!" shouted a Bad Boy sub, ready at the center faceoff circle. "Get a man in here!"

"Kirby! Go!" shouted Marty. "You're in for Jamal on defense!"

Kirby grabbed his stick and leapt onto the playing area, giving Jamal five as they crossed paths. "Come on, Kirby, pick me up," Jamal said.

Kirby nodded, not even stopping to think that he'd concentrated all week on playing forward. He knew next to nothing about defense.

84

As if they knew that, the Bad Boys mounted a rush down his side. Two of them went by, one on either side of him, passing the puck around behind him before he knew what was happening.

"Come on!" Lainie yelled, after just barely managing to deflect the slap shot. "I need some help back here!"

Kirby felt himself go red under his face mask. But there was no time to feel embarrassed. He had to go after the puck! Moving quickly, he outhustled Spike for it and flipped it down-rink to Marty.

The pass hit right on Marty's stick as he flew by Killer, who was stuck to him like glue. Marty had him by a step and fired from midzone, sending it between the pads of the sprawling goalie. Score!

The half ended with the Skates swarming Marty, their hero. He had gotten them back into the game with his last-minute goal, just ahead of halftime.

"That was some pass, Kirby," he said, slapping Kirby five. "Guys, I think we've got a player here."

"Listen, you guys on defense have got to stand your ground," Lainie complained. "I'm getting killed out there."

"They're too much bigger than Jamal and Kirby," Marty said. "And Nick, you've got to stay back to help."

"But you guys weren't getting any shots off!" Nick protested.

"He's right," Marty said. "We need more muscle on defense and more speed on offense. Kirby, you ready to play forward?"

"Definitely!" Kirby said excitedly. It was the chance he'd been waiting for all week.

"Good. I'll put in some time on defense. I'm big enough to get in their way."

"Thank goodness," Lainie muttered, nodding in approval.

"Will you lay off?" Trevor told her.

Lainie blinked. "You're right," she said, backing off. "Sorry. I guess I'm a little scared is all. They shoot hard."

"It's okay," Marty said. "We're all a team, and that's how we win. Put your hands in here."

They all put their hands together and shouted, "Go . . . Skates!" It was time for the second half.

The new strategy worked, in a way. The Bad Boys had no success getting the puck past Marty, but on the other hand, Kirby and Trevor were unable to get off any good shots.

Actually Kirby never got to see much of the puck. Trevor, not knowing if Kirby was any good, was hogging the puck, and getting it stolen by the Bad Boys time after time.

"I'm open! I'm open!" Kirby would shout. But Trevor, when he could have easily passed to him, didn't even try. Instead, he took wild shots.

Kirby realized that if he was ever going to get a shot, he'd have to get the puck on his own. He decided to try to make a steal in the forward zone.

Before he could succeed, however, he was

subbed for, and Marty went back to playing forward, inserting Jamal on defense. Suddenly Kirby was back on the bench.

Then, about halfway through the period, Marty went down. He tripped over the same crack in the pavement that had surprised Trevor in the first half and landed hard on his right shoulder. He lay there on the asphalt, writhing in pain. Play came to an instant stop.

"My shoulder! My shoulder!" Marty was crying. His parents were kneeling down next to him in an instant, and other parents were asking everyone to back away and give them room.

"It might be dislocated," Mr. Bledsoe said. "We'd better get him to the emergency room. Can you get up, son?"

Marty got to his feet, still whimpering, his arm hanging limp, as the stunned Skates looked on silently. He skated over to the gate and got into his parents' car with them. The Bledsoes sped off.

"Whoa, man!" Trevor said. "Do you think he's going to be okay?"

"Marty'll be okay," Lainie said, sounding not too sure of herself. "The question is, will we be okay without him?"

They all looked at each other anxiously as the Bad Boys started calling to them to resume the game or forfeit.

Trevor took over as acting captain. "Okay, Kirby, you're in at forward again. Let's go. Let's win it for Marty!"

With a yell, they took their positions. The puck was dropped, and Trevor won the faceoff, sending it back to Nick at the blue line.

"Nick! Here!" Kirby shouted. "I'm open!"

Nick passed it toward him, but the Bad Boys had heard Kirby shouting. Spike intercepted the puck, speeding the other way.

Kirby leapt into action, skating so fast that he overtook Spike just as he raised his stick for a slap shot. Reaching underneath, Kirby swept the puck onto his stick, and Spike fired nothing but air!

Kirby was already across the blue line by the

time anyone realized what had happened. He skated straight in, then faked a shot just as Killer got to him. The Bad Boy captain tripped as he tried to block the shot, but Kirby had never intended to shoot. Not yet.

Now, with Killer on the ground and Trevor yelling for him to pass the puck, Kirby skated straight in on the goalie. Zigging and zagging, he got the goalie off balance, then flipped the puck over the Bad Boy's shoulder and into the net!

A wild cheer erupted from the E Street side of the parking lot. "That's my boy!" he heard his father shouting.

Kirby was mobbed by his teammates, and the whole pile of them fell on top of him in total happiness.

But the game wasn't over yet. There were still a few minutes left in which to win — or lose. Furious and stunned, the Bad Boys turned up the heat, mounting rush after rush at the Skates' goal. But Lainie was not about to give anything up. Not now. Not after they'd come this far. At the end of regulation time, the score was tied, 2–2.

"Five-minute overtime," Lainie called out, and the two teams formed up immediately. In the flurry that followed, both teams played carefully, making sure not to lose the game by being out of position. There were a lot of stoppages of play as players fired the puck down-rink or out of bounds. Then, with only seconds left, the Bad Boys mounted a two-on-one rush. Kirby was way down at the other end of the rink, but he raced back toward his own zone, hoping against hope that he wasn't too late.

Killer got off a slap shot. Lainie did a full split to block it, and the puck came out in front of the goal. But Spike was there, waiting. Lainie tried to get back into position, but Kirby could see that she would never be able to stop the next shot.

As Spike wound up for the slap shot, Kirby's instincts took over. Lunging forward with his stick, he reached out as far as he could. The tip of his stick fell just short of the puck. But as Spike's stick came down, it hit Kirby's stick instead of the puck. There was a loud crack, but no shot. Lainie sprang forward to cover the puck, and the game was saved!

"Time's up!" shouted one of the parents, who was acting as timekeeper. The overtime ended the way regulation had: 2–2, a tie.

There was the usual lineup and hand-slapping at the end, but the Bad Boys were in a foul mood. Kirby saw at least one of them spit on his hand before offering it. He pulled his own hand back, avoiding total gross-out. Then, his arms around his teammates shoulders, he skated back with them toward the sideline.

"We did it! We saved the game for Marty!" Jamal shouted happily.

"What are you so happy about?" Trevor asked. "Marty got hurt. And besides, we didn't win."

"We will next time," Lainie said confidently. "Soon as we get Marty back, we'll have a rematch. Next Saturday, same time, their team said."

"If we get Marty back by then," Nick corrected.

"If his shoulder is dislocated, won't that keep him out of action all summer?"

They broke up to greet their parents. Although she didn't say anything, Kirby sensed that his mother was troubled.

"Marty'll be okay," he assured her. "You'll see."

"I don't know, Kirby," his mom replied. "That could have just as easily been you. The pavement here is in very bad repair. That boy Trevor nearly hurt himself, too."

"It's not that bad, Mom — really!" With a sinking heart, Kirby could see that he wasn't convincing her. He could only hope that Marty wasn't too badly hurt and that his parents would let him play in the rematch.

He didn't even want to think about what his summer would be like if they refused to let him play.

8

Just as Kirby and his parents were coming home after the game, the phone rang. Kirby ran to answer it. It was Marty Bledsoe.

"So, did we win?" he wanted to know.

"Tied, 2–2," Kirby said. "Are you okay?"

"I'm talking to you, aren't I?"

"Yeah," Kirby said, smiling. Marty couldn't be too badly hurt if he was joking around. "So? Did you break your arm?"

"Nah. They thought my shoulder was dislocated, but it turned out it's only a bruise. It got all purple, though. Wait till you see it — it's really cool."

"Does it hurt?"

"Only when I move it. But I'm in a sling, so I don't move it very often."

"I — I guess that means you can't play with us next week," Kirby said.

"It's worse than that," Marty said, his joking tone turning dismal. "Here's the really bad news. When the town found out I hurt myself, they got all scared about people using the parking lot. My dad told them we weren't going to sue or anything, but they don't care. The mayor already told my dad he's going to ask the town council to lock the parking lot so no one can play."

"Oh, no!" Kirby's stomach knotted. "They can't do that!"

"Yeah, well, you try and stop them, because my dad couldn't. And he's a lawyer." Marty sure sounded down about it.

"Hey, Marty?" Kirby asked, a thought suddenly striking him. "How come you called me first, and not any of the others?"

"Huh? I don't know," Marty confessed. "I guess . . . I guess I wanted to see how it was going for my new teammate. And I don't know — about the lot being closed, I thought you might have an idea or something. I already know what the others are going to say about it."

"Like . . . ?"

"Like Trevor will start getting himself all upset, Lainie will throw a fit, Nick will cry, and Jamal will secretly be happy he doesn't have to get out there and face the Bad Boys again."

Kirby laughed. "So what do you want to do?"

"I need to rest," Marty said. "They gave me something at the hospital for the pain, and I'm kind of out of it. Could you call everybody, and tell them to meet on E Street tomorrow at two? We need to figure something out."

"Okay. See you then," Kirby said, and hung up.

"What was that all about?" his dad asked, peeking over the top of his newspaper.

"Marty's okay," Kirby said, and explained about his shoulder being bruised, not dislocated. "I've got to make some calls, all right?"

He ran upstairs to call the others from the phone in his mom's office. Kirby wasn't sure he wanted to tell his parents about the parking lot thing. Not until after the meeting, anyway. Whatever happened, he didn't want to do anything else to get them upset about roller hockey. Things were touchy enough already.

The E Street Skates sat on the curb in a row. Most of them were wearing their skates, except Marty, who had walked, and Kirby, who had biked over. Marty had his right arm in a blue cloth sling. Everyone wore serious expressions on their faces. Nobody was saying a word.

"This really bites," Trevor finally said.

"You can say that again," Lainie agreed. "There's got to be something we can do about it! I mean, this is supposed to be a democracy, right? That parking lot should be of the people, by the people, and for the people, right?"

"What are you, Lincoln?" Trevor said with a little smile. They all laughed — the first time they'd laughed in the whole hour they'd been sitting there.

"Shut up," Lainie said, giving Trevor a playful

elbow in the arm. "Seriously, we're citizens in this town, aren't we? Just because we're kids and we don't vote, does that mean we don't count for anything? How can they do this to us?"

"It's called lawsuits, Lainie," Jamal said. "Somebody could sue the town for a lot of money. Marty, for instance." He rubbed his hands together and licked his lips greedily. "I'd be happy to be your lawyer, old pal!"

"Quit the clowning," Marty said. "But you're right — that's why they're not letting us play."

"Is there anyplace else we could go for games?" Kirby asked.

Everyone shook their heads. "That's the whole trouble with this town," Nick said disgustedly. "They never do anything cool for kids."

"What about the May Fair?" Marty asked. "And the soccer league and the town pool? They do stuff. They just hate it when kids skate, that's all."

"It's discrimination!" Lainie shouted. "I say we talk to the mayor!"

"And tell him what?" Trevor asked. "That we demand a skating rink? Yeah, he'll really buy that because we said so."

"Wait a minute," Kirby said. "The mayor should at least hear our side. Maybe we can convince him we're right."

"Yeah, right," Trevor said skeptically.

"Hey, it's worth a try," Marty said. "Nobody's got any other ideas, and it's better than doing nothing."

"So what are our arguments?" Kirby asked.

"Well, that we need a rink, and the parking lot's perfect for it . . . ," Lainie began.

"But he'll say the pavement's too messed up and that it's dangerous for kids." Marty held up his wounded arm to prove his point. "He'll say we'd need insurance or something."

"So the lot would need to be paved," Kirby reasoned.

"Right. Which would cost like a zillion dollars," Nick said, sighing. "And then you'd still have to get insurance. That costs money too."

"Well, maybe we could get the town to pay for it," Kirby said.

Trevor shook his head. "The mayor's not going to listen when a bunch of kids come in to see him. It'll be like, 'Oh, that's nice, children. Go and play now. But not in the parking lot.' "

"Well, then, how about we make a petition?" Jamal said.

"What's a petition?" Nick asked.

"Nick, everyone knows what a petition is!" Trevor said, rolling his eyes. "It's when you get people's signatures in favor of whatever, and hand it in."

"So, like, we get a hundred signatures, and then we give it to the mayor?" Nick asked, beginning to smile.

"A hundred? Try a thousand!" Lainie said excitedly. "Come on, gang, let's go back to my house and write up our statement! We're not stopping until we get our rink!"

We, the people of Valemont, hereby demand that the parking lot of the former cardboard box factory be repaved immediately and that the citizens of Valemont have free use of the lot for adult-supervised activities, such as roller hockey, until such time as the property is sold.

The petition was ready for signing. Mr. Bledsoe had gone over it and approved it. He'd made copies of it for all the members of the team. They were just about to go back out into the street to start getting signatures, when Kirby suddenly realized something.

"You know what, guys — we're forgetting some people here."

"Who?" Nick asked. But Marty and Lainie were already nodding in agreement.

"The Bates Avenue Bad Boys," Marty said. "You're right, Kirby. We may hate their guts, but we need their help for this. We've got to get them involved in the petition drive if we're going to get a thousand signatures."

"Well, I'm not going over there," Jamal said, crossing his arms.

"Me neither," Nick said. "Those guys will just beat us up."

"Fine, we'll go without you," Lainie said. "But they're going to want the lot paved and opened, too."

"I can't go right now," Trevor said. "My cousins are over for Sunday dinner."

"And I've got to stay off my skates for now," Marty said.

"Well, I guess it's just me and Kirby," Lainie said. "No problem."

"Don't do it, Lainie!" Jamal protested. "Those guys will eat you two for lunch."

"I'm not afraid of them, and neither is Kirby," Lainie responded. "Are you, Kirby?"

"Nope," Kirby lied. He was terrified, but he wasn't going to say so.

"You're sure?" Marty said. "Maybe I'll walk over and meet you there."

"You wouldn't be much good in a fight," Lainie said, flicking a finger at his sling strap. "Thanks, anyway. Come on, Kirby."

As she skated and Kirby rode toward Bates Avenue, Kirby looked over at Lainie. "You're really not scared?" he asked her.

" 'Course I am. Are you crazy?" she replied. "Aren't you?"

"Yup."

"Well, do your best to hide it, because here we are," Lainie said. "Follow me."

The Bad Boys were practicing as usual. As Lainie and Kirby approached, one of them delivered an illegal body check to another. The second boy slammed into a parked car, denting it a little.

"Yeah! Yeah! I decked you, Slater!" Killer's voice rang out. "In your face!"

Slater dragged himself back up and shook himself off. "Hey," he said, "look who's here."

"Whoa, it's the geek and his girlfriend! Wanna play a pickup game? No adults around to protect you now!"

"We've got something more important to talk about," Lainie said simply.

"Oh, yeah? Like what?" All the Bad Boys were gathering around now. Lainie handed Killer a copy of the petition.

"This," Lainie said. "We're circulating a petition to hand in to the mayor, to get him to pave the parking lot and let us skate there again."

Killer stared at the page and nodded. " 'We, the people . . .' Not bad. You make this up?" he asked.

"Uh-huh. We need your help getting signatures. At least a thousand by next week."

Killer spit on the ground. "No problem," he

said. "We're gonna get way more signatures than you losers."

"In your dreams," Lainie said, tossing her hair back off her forehead.

"We'll see," Killer said. "Hey, guys, go get everyone you see to sign one of these papers. If they won't sign, break their necks." He grinned and looked at Lainie. "Salesmanship," he said. "Now, get out of here, and take your geek boyfriend with you. Got it?"

Lainie narrowed her eyes dangerously but didn't answer. Instead, she said, "Come on, Kirby," and started skating away. Kirby followed her before the Bad Boys decided to chase them.

"That was cool!" he said. "You were so awesome, Lainie!"

Lainie grinned. "Thanks," she said. "I thought I was pretty good, too. Now let's see if those jerks manage to get any signatures. They're not going to get more than us, that's for sure. Not if I have to spend every last minute this week on it."

"Me, too!" Kirby said. He really admired Lainie. She sure was brave. Even though she'd admitted to him that she was afraid, she never let the Bad Boys know it. Kirby was sure his own teeth had been chattering the whole time.

Kirby was shy at first about ringing the doorbells of people he didn't know. And when they opened their doors, he stumbled on the speech he'd prepared. But after Marty called him and it turned out that he was having the same problem, Kirby didn't feel so bad. At least he wasn't the only one.

So the two boys worked out a plan. They would set up a table outside Reilly's Sporting Goods, downtown. Lots of people came by there, and the ones who went into Reilly's were already interested in sports. There would be a poster asking people to sign the petition, so all he and Marty would have to do would be to answer questions.

This plan turned out to be a big success. After

only fifteen minutes, they had gathered twenty signatures! Seeing the crowd gathering in front of his store, Mr. Reilly came out to see what was happening.

"What's this you're up to?" he asked, looking over the poster they'd hand-painted. "'Help make the roller hockey rink a reality'? What roller hockey rink?"

"The parking lot at the old cardboard box factory," Marty explained. "We want the town to pave it and insure it so that kids can play there."

"Well, I think that's a great idea!" Mr. Reilly said. "This town doesn't pay enough attention to recreation for kids, if you ask me! Besides, it'll help me sell more sports equipment. Where do I sign?"

Kirby showed him where, and Mr. Reilly signed with a flourish. "There! Now, let me know if there's anything else I can do to help." Turning to the people walking down the street, he shouted, "Hey, everyone! Come and look at this!"

Marty gave Kirby the thumbs-up sign, along with a big smile. "Yes!" he whispered.

"Well, isn't this something! Over one thousand signatures!" Mayor Casper Huggins rubbed a hand over his shiny bald head in wonderment. "There are only five thousand people in all of Valemont — that's one in five . . . twenty percent — my, my!"

Kirby could almost see the mayor calculating votes in the next election.

"Six hundred twenty-seven of the signatures came from us," Lainie whispered to Kirby just loud enough for the Bad Boys, sitting across the aisle of the town council chamber, to hear. The Bad Boys sat there and smoldered.

At the front of the room, Marty and Killer had just handed over the petition. Now, as they returned to their seats, the five town council members gathered around and read Lainie's statement. They nodded, impressed.

"I move we vote on this," said one council member, taking off her glasses.

"I second the motion," said another, raising his hand.

The vote was unanimous, and everyone in the crowd cheered. Every member of both teams was there, along with at least half the parents. Hockey was a big issue in their families; Kirby could see that. And so could the council.

"Ahem," Mayor Huggins said, "can we please have quiet? Thank you. Now, the council has voted in favor of the proposition. I therefore proclaim that the parking lot be paved and temporarily put at the disposal of Valemont's citizens, for their supervised use — subject to the insurer's approval, and funding, of course." He cleared his throat again and sat down. "Anything else before we adjourn this meeting?" he asked.

"I have a question," Lainie got up and said. Everyone looked at her, including Kirby. "Does what you just said mean that we have to pay for it ourselves?"

"Ahem," Mayor Huggins coughed as murmuring rose in the room. "Well, yes . . . of course, the town budget has no provision for this. I can't direct town personnel to make the improvements without assuring them of payment."

"Well, how much will it cost?" Mr. Bledsoe asked from his seat.

"Ahem, well, let's see . . . somewhere in the neighborhood of five thousand dollars, plus another thousand for insurance."

"Six thousand dollars!?" The murmur in the room became a roar, as people leapt to their feet.

"I'm willing to make a personal contribution to begin the collection of funds," the mayor said hurriedly. Kirby was new in town, but even he knew there was an election coming up that November, and that the mayor was running for reelection. "I pledge five hundred dollars!" he said.

Everyone cheered. "Count me in for two-fifty!" Mr. Bledsoe shouted, to more applause. Ten minutes later, the amount needed had shrunk to only three thousand dollars.

"We can do this," Lainie said, turning to her teammates. "We got signatures — all we have to do is go around asking for money. Easy!"

"Nuh-uh," Jamal said. "Asking for money is harder. Why don't we have a yard sale or something?"

"I could bake some things, and you could have a bake sale!" Kirby's mom volunteered.

Kirby's heart swelled in his chest as all the other kids thanked his mom. Kirby gave her a big hug.

"We could sell lemonade," Jamal suggested.

"How about a car wash?" Kirby was startled to hear Killer's voice in his ear. The big brute's arm went around Kirby's shoulder. "We can do this," Killer said, smiling at the E Street Skates.

Lainie smiled broadly. "Guys," she said, "this is going to be a breeze!"

It wasn't a breeze. Nothing like one. It was two weeks of backbreaking, sweaty work. But none of the Skates or the Bad Boys complained. They could all see the money adding up, quarter by quarter, dollar by dollar.

Through the car wash, the yard sale, and the bake sale, Kirby met a lot of people in town.

Of course, there were some people who didn't want to help out, either because they thought the paving should be paid for by whoever wanted to use the lot or because they thought skaters were a nuisance. But most people gave at least a little to the cause. They seemed to like the idea of young people trying to do something good for themselves and the town.

It was the hottest time of the summer, though, and that wound up being the hard part. Kirby would come home exhausted after taking his turn working at the bake sale or yard sale or car wash. Sometimes he'd take a shower, but other times, he was too tired even for that and just flopped down on his bed to rest.

By the end of the second week, they had done it. Three thousand dollars in cash had been raised. When they all showed up at the weekly town council meeting and handed the money over to the mayor, he was speechless — which was saying a lot for Mayor Huggins.

After a few seconds, he managed to say, "I'm — I am — what a surprise! I congratulate all of you; you've done an — an outstanding job!" Turning to his town council, he added, "I want this work done as soon as possible! When can we start?"

"Tomorrow," one of the council members replied. "I'll get a work crew on it first thing in the morning."

"Splendid!" Mayor Huggins was beaming.

"Again, let me congratulate you all. You have done Valemont a great service. Your town thanks you, and I thank you."

Three days later, the parking lot had been cleaned of all litter and freshly, beautifully paved. Instead of white lines for parking spaces, the town had actually painted a hockey rink — complete with faceoff circles, goal creases, and a blue line across the center!

Gathering for their first game on the new rink, the E Street Skates stood opposite the Bates Avenue Bad Boys.

"Hey, you!" Lainie yelled at one of the Bad Boys as the two teams prepared for the big game. "Don't spit out your gum here. You're ruining our new rink! What's wrong with you?"

"Oh. Sorry," the player said, and picked it up, not even giving Lainie an argument.

Boy, Kirby thought, Lainie sure is tough. When she gives orders, people listen. He wished he was more like that.

Marty was there with his parents, but he wasn't in uniform, and he wasn't playing. His shoulder had healed — mostly. But the doctor and Marty's parents were not ready to let him take a chance of hurting it again so soon.

Marty had told the Skates he'd be ready in about another week. For now, he could coach them, but they were going to have to beat the Bad Boys without him in the lineup.

That wasn't going to be easy, either. The Bad Boys were really charged up. Not only had they failed to beat the Skates last time, but the Skates had gotten more signatures and raised more money than they had.

The Skates tested the new surface for a while, getting used to the feel of the pavement. Then Marty brought them into a pregame huddle. "Okay, guys. They're probably going to come out playing rough and trying to scare us. But we've got a big audience today," he said, indicating the crowd that was congregated outside the rink's boundaries. "So if the Bad Boys do anything more than touch you, be sure to scream like you're in extreme agony, and I bet the adults will make them stop. Other than that, Trevor, you need to keep an eye out for Kirby. They're expecting you to take all the shots. So if they double-team you, Kirby will be free."

"Okay," Trevor said, frowning. "But don't worry, I'll be able to get the shots off."

"Maybe," Marty said. "Nick, you have to stay back the whole time. No more two-on-one rushes for them, okay?"

"Okay."

"Okay, then, let's go. Put your hands in here."

They did their "Go . . . Skates!" cheer, then went out to face off with the Bad Boys.

For the first five minutes or so, the game stayed scoreless. Trevor was hogging the puck as usual. Even when Kirby's man came over to double-team him, Trevor didn't try to pass to Kirby. Instead, he fired off a quick shot at the goal, which the goalie easily handled.

On the other end, the defense was playing better. Jamal had new skates, and both he and Nick were having an easier time skating on the new, smoother surface.

Finally Spike took a shot that ricocheted off Jamal's stick and straight past Lainie into the goal. That broke the scoreless tie, and it meant the Skates would have to come from behind.

Kirby decided that Trevor wasn't ever going to pass it to him. In which case, Kirby wasn't going to wait around for the pass to come. Instead, when his man left to double-team Trevor on the other side of the forward zone, Kirby headed straight for the goal crease and stood there, waiting for Trevor's inevitable shot.

When the shot caromed off the goalie's blocking pad, Kirby was ready. All he had to do was guide the puck back into the net! As the Bad Boys' goalie stood in shock, Kirby jumped so high in the air that he felt like he was flying. The Skates all mobbed him, slapping him on the back and on the helmet and yelling their heads off.

It was Kirby's second goal as an E Street Skate.

And he'd hardly even touched the puck!

"Way to go, Kirby!" he heard his mother shouting from the sideline. "Whoo-oo!"

"All right!" Marty said, giving him a high five. In a low voice he added, "Listen, Kirby, keep going to the goal, because Trevor's never going to change."

"Right," Kirby said, flashing a huge grin.

"Let's see if we can catch them off guard again." Marty slapped him on the back and sent him over to the faceoff circle.

The Bad Boys scored once more, right before halftime, on an awesome slap shot from Killer. Lainie flinched in spite of herself, and the puck went in, just over her shoulder.

"Don't feel bad, Lainie," Kirby told her at halftime as they cooled down by pouring water over their heads. "That goal would have gone by anybody."

"I should have had it," Lainie insisted. She slammed her stick on the ground.

In the second half, the Skates rallied. Trevor,

angry at being pushed around by the Bad Boys' defensemen, whipped a slap shot by their goalie. That tied the game, and Trevor loved every minute of it. This was his chance to gloat, and he took it.

"In your face!" he said, pointing at the defenders, who nearly lost it when they heard that. They glared at Trevor with pure fury in their eyes.

"Shut up, punk!" Killer shouted, and Spike had to hold him back.

"Do it in the game," Kirby overheard him say in Killer's ear. "Wait for your moment."

The game grew tense. Everyone knew that a fight could start at any moment. Then, very late in the game, one of the Bad Boy defenders saw that Trevor was looking the other way. He quickly gave him a sharp elbow in the back.

"Ow!" Trevor yelled. "Hey, come on! That's a penalty!"

But there was no referee to call penalties. It had always been understood that if anyone did anything outrageous, they were penalized by common agreement. But this time, the Bad Boy defender just shook his head and went back to work.

Trevor was really fuming now. In spite of Marty's warning to take it easy, he couldn't resist getting even. Next time he got the puck, he tried skating right through the defense and got into it with his shoulder first.

"That's a definite penalty!" Killer yelled, staring straight at Marty.

Marty nodded, disgusted. "You're off, Trevor."

"What!?" Trevor was beside himself.

"You checked him. You're off."

"But he elbowed me first!"

"Nobody saw it," Marty said. "Sorry."

"Man," Trevor steamed. "We need a ref around here."

Kirby agreed. "Maybe one of the parents could do it," he suggested. But no one agreed with him. A ref would need to be impartial, they all said, and on skates besides.

Trevor skated to the penalty box, fighting back

angry tears, while the Bad Boys hooted and cheered.

This was the chance Bates Avenue had been waiting for. Without Trevor to fear, they sent one of their defensemen down the rink with the forwards in a power play, forcing Kirby to play defense, too.

With the puck in the Skates' zone, the Bad Boys' goalie came out of the game and was replaced with yet another forward. This gave the Bad Boys a two-player advantage, and the Skates just couldn't stop the avalanche of shots. One of them finally beat Lainie, and the Bad Boys led again, 3–2.

"One minute left!" Marty shouted. "Let's get it back!" The Skates quickly managed to force a faceoff in the Bad Boys' zone. With half a minute left, Lainie shed her goalie gear, grabbed a forward's stick, and skated back on the ice as an attacker, leaving the Skates' goal mouth empty. It was a big risk, but it had to be taken.

Unfortunately Lainie sent a pass back to Nick

that went over his stick. The puck rolled on its edge right down the rink and into the Skates' empty goal — just as the final whistle blew! Final score: Bates Avenue 4, E Street 2.

"We win!" the Bad Boys all bellowed, slamming bodies with each other. "Yeah! Yeah! World champs! All right!"

"What a bunch of jerks," Kirby heard Marty say under his breath.

"We would never have lost if you were playing," Trevor retorted bitterly.

"Yeah," Marty said, "well, we'll get our chance next week. And I'll be playing. I promise you that. This thing isn't over. Now that we've got our new rink, it's going to be a long, tough season. We'll see who's on top when it's over."

Kirby was excited, in spite of the fact that they'd lost. He couldn't wait for the next game the following Saturday. Now that they had the new rink to practice on, he could skate with the team every day!

11

The next day, the Skates met at the rink for their regular practice. The two teams had worked out a schedule. But instead of playing, the Skates devoted most of the time to talking things over.

"I should be able to play by next weekend," Marty told them. "But if we're going to play the Bad Boys anymore, we'd better find a referee."

"You said it!" Trevor agreed hotly. "I'm not taking any more of that stuff from them. If they try anything, I'll —"

"Great, that's all we need is a big fight," Lainie chimed in. "Then the mayor will step in and close us down. Good idea, Trevor — not."

"Lainie's right," Jamal said. "But where are we going to find a ref?"

"Maybe some high school kids would do it," Nick suggested. "If we pay them a little."

"Where are we going to get the money?" Jamal asked.

"We could sell lemonade and stuff at our games," Kirby suggested. "If we get enough people there, it would pay for a ref."

"We could put up posters and sell tickets, too," Nick suggested. "But with so few kids around, I don't know . . ."

"We'll never get enough people," Trevor said disconsolately. "All the kids around here are either in the game or off at camp for the summer."

"You know," Kirby said, "I can't help thinking there must be other kids somewhere — maybe not around here, but in other towns nearby. Maybe they're into hockey, too. Maybe they'd like to come see us play."

"Yeah," Lainie said. "Maybe their parents will drive them all the way here just to get rid of them for a couple hours!"

They all laughed, but Kirby was serious. "No, I

mean it," he said. "I'll bet there are other hockey teams out there somewhere. Wouldn't it be great to play against a normal team for once, instead of getting beat up all the time by Killer and Spike and those guys?"

"Hey! I've got an idea!" Jamal suddenly said. "I've got an E-mail buddy over in Bakersville who plays roller hockey on a team. Now that we've got a rink, maybe they would come and watch us play."

"Why would they do that?" Nick asked. "Just to sit there and cheer?"

"We could let them play the winners!" Jamal said triumphantly. "Two games, twice as much lemonade sold!"

"That's a fantastic idea!" Marty said excitedly. "Hey, maybe we'll even get a league going. Then we wouldn't get stuck playing the Bad Boys every time."

"What do you mean?" Trevor said, still smarting. "I *want* to play them! I want to stick it to them good!"

"As long as there's a referee, Trev," Marty cautioned. "Remember, if we get into a fight, the town might take away our privileges here."

"I know, I know," Trevor muttered. "So where are we gonna find a ref?"

"Let's put up a want ad!" Kirby suggested. "Reilly's Sporting Goods has a bulletin board, and there's one at the bank, too!"

No sooner said than done. The ads were up by Tuesday, and by Thursday, they had their referee — Clayton Brown, who'd be a junior at the high school in the fall and was spending the summer working at Reilly's.

There was only one problem — he wasn't available this coming Saturday. "I've got my cousin's wedding in Woodford," he explained. "You guys still want me for the next weekend?"

"Sure!" they all said. They didn't have much choice. Clayton was the only person who'd responded to their ad.

Meanwhile, Jamal's E-mail buddy, Chris

Cosmillo, and his team from Bakersville, agreed to come watch them play on Saturday and to play the winner afterward.

All they had to do now was make the lemonade!

When Saturday came, the rink was crowded. Besides the two teams and their families, the team from Bakersville had also shown up, wearing fluorescent orange uniforms that said *Rocky Raccoons* in black lettering.

Seeing them, Killer skated over to Marty, who was standing with Kirby, both of them all suited up and ready to play.

"Who do those clowns think they are, showing up here in uniform like that?" Killer asked Marty. "This is *our* rink, not theirs. They don't even live around here."

"They're from Bakersville," Marty told him.

"We invited them to watch," Kirby added. "And to play the winner."

"Oh, yeah?" Killer said with a scowl. "Who told you you could do that?"

"We didn't figure we needed your permission," Marty said flatly. "Anyway, we're going to beat you, so don't let it bother you."

"Like fun, you are," Killer shot back. "We'll wipe the floor with you guys, and then we'll take care of them." He turned and skated away, motioning to his team to join him at the faceoff circle.

"Great," Marty said. "Now we've got them mad, and we haven't even started."

Sure enough, the Bad Boys played their roughest game yet. It seemed like they were deliberately trying to hit Marty's bad shoulder. Marty managed to avoid reinjuring it, but he had to take it easy in order to protect it. That made him less effective.

Trevor kept taking wild shots at the goal, even from impossible angles. He hogged the puck worse than ever, never letting Kirby get off a shot, though he did get open a few times.

The Bad Boys crowded the Skates' goal crease

time after time, pushing Jamal and Nick around. Even Lainie got a few scrapes and bruises.

The game ended with another Bad Boy victory — 3 to zip. Afterward, Jamal's friend Chris came over to the Skates, holding a cup of lemonade. "Listen," he said. "We're not playing those guys. No way. Not without a referee."

"But we've got a ref!" Nick said, then stopped himself. "Next week, that is."

"Well, we'll have to play next week, then," Chris said. "I'm not going anywhere near those guys without a ref. They play dirty."

"Tell us about it," Marty agreed. "But don't worry. There'll be a ref here. We're paying for him. That lemonade you're drinking? That's his salary."

Chris finished his drink and nodded. "No wonder it was so expensive," he said. "Okay, see you next week. And he'd better be here, or we're gone."

"You got it," Marty promised. And as Chris

moved off again, he muttered, "Boy, I sure hope Clayton shows up."

Clayton Brown had played ice hockey at the high school for two seasons. At six feet tall and over two hundred pounds, he was big enough to break up any fight, Kirby noted with satisfaction. He had agreed to referee for a modest fee. Even better, he had shown up on time, whistle, black-and-white-striped shirt, and all.

He introduced himself to all the members of both teams, while about thirty fans, including the Rocky Raccoons, sat on the sidelines, sipping lemonade and munching on cookies, this week's new fund-raising addition.

"This is going to be awesome!" Kirby whispered as he and the other E Street Skates stood at the center faceoff circle.

"You can say that again!" Marty whispered back. "But to make it really awesome, we've got to beat the Bad Boys."

"We're going to," Lainie said. "No way I'm going to let them score."

"I'm going to pepper them with so many shots they won't know what hit them!" Trevor said.

The ref blew his whistle, and the players gathered for the opening faceoff. Killer looked straight into Marty's eyes and said, "I hope your shoulder's ready."

For a second, Kirby wondered if he meant it in a friendly way or if it was more of a threat. The look in Killer's eyes gave him his answer.

For this game, Marty had decided to play defense. That meant Kirby would start the game as a forward, taking Marty's old spot. Nobody argued with the decision, not even Jamal, who had to start the game on the bench as a sub.

So after the Bad Boys took the faceoff, Marty dropped back. With his big, athletic body and good speed facing them, the Bad Boys were unable to muscle through to get off any good shots at Lainie. Meanwhile, Marty kept knocking the puck off their sticks and sending it toward Trevor and Kirby. Yes, Kirby, thought. Marty was definitely completely healthy again.

But every time Kirby got the puck on his stick, the Bad Boy defender would rush right at him, forcing him to twist and turn out of the way. Kirby wasn't able to control the puck while doing it. Three times, the defender actually ran into Kirby. That got Trevor and the other Skates yelling at the referee to call a penalty for bodychecking.

The referee refused to whistle it, though. "He was going for the puck, not the body," he insisted, motioning for the teams to keep playing.

Kirby's bruises were real, though. And he knew that the hits were intentional. The Bad Boys were trying to intimidate the new guy, the little kid — the geek. It made him mad, and every time his arm or leg ached, it made him madder.

Seeing that the referee wasn't going to call the penalties for banging into the other team, the Bad Boys just got rougher. It was what they did best; never mind that it was against the rules. The crowd was roaring — some in protest of the rough play, some in support of the Bad Boys. Kirby guessed that those would be their parents.

Once again, Marty got Kirby the puck. And again, the defender came up and knocked Kirby down.

"Come on, ref! Where's the penalty?" Trevor screamed, but the ref just shook his head.

As Kirby got to his feet again, he could see Marty rushing madly at the kid who'd knocked Kirby over.

"Marty! No!" Kirby shouted. But it was too late. Marty barreled into the kid from behind, sending him flying forward. The whistle blew long and loud, and the ref pointed right at Marty.

"No!" Marty yelled. "No, no, no! He hit our guy first!"

"I saw you," the ref said. "I didn't see him. Two minutes for roughing."

Marty slammed his stick down so hard that it broke, and headed for the sideline. Jamal skated up to him and squeezed his shoulder. "Don't worry, Marty," he said. "We'll take care of them."

Jamal had the heart of a great hockey player, all right. Unfortunately his athletic skills were not the greatest. The Bad Boys took quick advantage of Marty's absence. Less than a minute into his penalty, they finally whacked the puck past Lainie into the net, after a seven-shot barrage.

Lainie slammed her stick into the net in fury. "Your fault, ref!" she shouted. "Get some glasses, huh?"

The ref's face reddened in anger and embarrassment. "Hey, I'm just trying to let you guys play instead of stopping the game every two minutes," he said. "But if that's what you want, you got it!" He skated away. Watching it all, Kirby wondered what the Rocky Raccoons thought about this referee so far. From the looks on their faces, they didn't think much of him. For that matter, neither did Kirby. Too bad he was the only one they had.

Marty came back into the game. But now everyone was being a lot more careful because they knew that the ref was just itching to blow his whistle the first time anybody even touched anybody else.

That made it easier for Kirby to skate. And when he could skate, he could do it faster than anyone else on either team. He gave the defenders fits as he darted in and out between them, always looking for the pass from Trevor.

But Trevor, as usual, and especially when he was angry, was shooting every time he got the puck. Kirby had to concentrate on being in the right place to get a rebound off one of Trevor's shots.

Seeing this, Marty called out, "Pass, Trevor!"

Trevor turned and cupped his hand to his ear. "What?"

"Pass!"

Trevor shrugged, unable to hear over the roar of the crowd. Marty grabbed the puck off Spike's stick and skated forward with it until he was close to Trevor. "Pass the puck to Kirby," he said. "He's open. Look for him."

"Yeah, okay," Trevor said. Just as he said it, Killer came up behind Marty and stole the puck from him, heading back down-rink with it. Spike was with him on the right wing, and before Marty could get back, both Bad Boys had passed Nick and had a free rush at Lainie.

Killer wound up at close range and fired a shot that hit Lainie square in the helmet. She went down, stunned for a moment, as Spike flicked in the easy rebound for another score.

The halftime whistle blew moments later, with the score at Bad Boys 2, Skates 0. "Same old story," Killer mocked as he skated by the Skates' bench. "With a referee or without."

"Let me at him," Trevor steamed, but Marty forced him back down on the bench.

"Will you get ahold of yourself?" Marty told him. "We've got to play our game. We can't let the Bad Boys upset us so we start playing like them."

"Yeah, we could never be as good at being jerks as they are," Lainie cracked.

Kirby just sat there, breathing hard, exhausted and hurting.

"You okay?" Jamal asked him. "They beat you up pretty bad."

"My mom's never going to let me play again," Kirby said. "I keep telling her it's a noncontact sport."

"Well, it's supposed to be," Nick said, shrugging. "Those guys just don't play fair."

"Yeah, and that ref is letting them get away with it!" Lainie said. "He cost us that first goal, you know."

"I know," Marty agreed. "But we can't let that rattle us. We've got one half to go, and we're two goals down. We need a plan to get back in this game."

As Marty sketched plays with his finger on the ground, Kirby looked up and saw that the ref was arguing with some of the Skates' parents — including his own. His mom and dad looked angry, and when Kirby's mom looked over at him, he motioned for her not to get the ref mad.

Kirby read his mom's lips. She was asking him if he was okay. He nodded vigorously to show that he was. She nodded back, concerned but looking a little relieved.

"So that's how we do it, okay?" Marty said. "Put your hands in here. We're going to show those guys what the sport of roller hockey is all about."

They gave their Skates cheer, then skated out for the second half, determined to come back and win.

The puck was dropped. The second half began. This time, Nick was on the bench, with Jamal taking his place in the defensive zone. Quickly the Bad Boys mounted a rush, double-teaming on Jamal's side.

But Jamal, trying to protect himself from the attack, somehow got his stick on the puck and knocked it away from Spike. The puck rolled on its edge right onto Marty's stick. He passed it up to Trevor, then skated forward into the offensive zone.

This was the Skates' new second-half strategy. Since they were losing, they had to gamble, throwing everything they had at the Bad Boys' goal. If they failed, they'd lose the game by a lopsided score. On the other hand, if they succeeded, they could come from behind.

Trevor skated in, then left the puck for Marty. Marty took it, faked a shot, then passed it over to Kirby without even looking at him. Kirby wound up for a quick shot.

But Killer had not been sitting around looking surprised all this time. Hurrying back into his own defensive zone, his eyes flashed from Kirby standing there to Marty with the puck. He got to Kirby just as Kirby was about to shoot, reached out his stick, and pulled Kirby's feet out from under him.

Kirby fell forward, his stick in the air, and hit the pavement smack on the front of his helmet. He was so stunned, he didn't even hear the referee blow his whistle, calling a penalty on Killer for tripping.

Marty and Trevor came over and kneeled at Kirby's side. "You okay?" Marty asked. Kirby sort of heard him and knew he was supposed to answer. But he couldn't get the words out. Marty and Trevor helped him to his feet and guided him to the sideline, one of them supporting him on each side.

Kirby sat down and put his head between his legs. He took off his helmet and breathed deeply, trying to get his senses back. His mom and dad were with him now, he noticed, and his mom was rubbing his back the way she did when he felt nauseated.

He didn't feel nauseated now, though. In fact, he was already feeling better. And when a cheer went up from the crowd and he heard Trevor yell, "Yeah! Way to go, Marty!" he knew that his team had scored and that they were back in the game again.

Midway through the second half, with the score still 2–1 in favor of the Bad Boys, Marty called time out, and the team headed for the bench. "Kirby," Marty said, "you ready to come back in?"

"I think so," Kirby said. "Yeah, sure. I'm ready."

"Good man," Marty said. "Here's what we're

going to do. We're going to do a line change on the fly. Next time we get possession in our zone, Nick, you get the puck to me and then head to the bench. When he gets within ten feet, Kirby, you hop out onto the rink, and I'll feed you the puck for a clean breakaway."

"Got it," Kirby said.

"Got it," Nick echoed.

"Good. Let's do it," Marty said as they headed back out.

Playing decoy, Trevor lost the puck on purpose. As planned, the Bad Boys got excited at their sudden scoring chance, sending one of their defenders into the forward zone. Nick managed to steal the puck from him when Killer made a drop pass. Then Nick fed Marty and headed for the sideline. Nobody followed him. The Bad Boys were all concentrating on Marty.

"Go for it!" Nick whispered as Kirby jumped onto the rink surface. At that precise moment, Marty fed him the puck — a long, perfect pass. Kirby grabbed it.

Only one defender stood between him and the goal. Instead of trying to fake him out — that was how Kirby had kept losing the puck in the first half — he tried simply outracing him. Kirby went around the player's right side. Sure enough, the big, lumbering defenseman could not keep up.

Kirby could hear the Bad Boys yelling, and it made him glad. He focused like a laser on the spot he wanted to shoot for, then let the puck fly.

Bull's-eye! Score! Tie game!

The next thing Kirby knew, he was being mobbed by his teammates. They had done it! They had tied the game. But, as Marty soon reminded them, they had one more goal to score.

Now both teams were playing recklessly, trying to score that one final goal that would be the nail in the other team's coffin. Kirby barely saw the puck as each team's scoring stars tried to win the game all by themselves.

Seeing the Bad Boys all rushing the Skates' zone, Kirby went back to help out on defense. Killer, almost all the way back at the blue line, let a shot fly. Lainie just managed to make the save, and the puck rolled out again — past Marty, past Nick, past the Bad Boys — all the way to Kirby.

Feeling his heart leap into his throat, Kirby took off the other way. Nobody was back on defense!

Now, Killer came from the other side of the rink, trying to cut Kirby off before he could get a shot away. Just as he got there, Kirby fed the puck a little ahead of himself, then did a full 360-degree spin.

This move surprised Killer so much so that he tripped over his own skates and fell to the ground at Kirby's feet! Kirby leapt over his prone body, grabbed the puck, and with a big smile, let loose a stinging shot.

The goalie tried in vain to get a glove on it, but the puck was speeding too fast. The puck hit the back of the net — score! Seconds later, the ref blew his whistle three times. Time was up. The big game was over!

The Skates mobbed Kirby yet again and carried him off the rink on their shoulders, chanting his name: "Kir-by! Kir-by! Kir-by!"

His parents came up and hugged him, too. "I'm so proud of you, son!" his dad said.

"Is your head okay?" his mom wanted to know. But even she was smiling, though her eyes were concerned.

Looking across to the other side of the rink, Kirby could see the Bad Boys shoving each other angrily, blaming each other for the defeat. Kirby shook his head. He hoped they would learn one day that friendship was more important than winning or losing.

Still, it sure felt great to win. And on top of it, he was the hero of the game! And it had happened exactly the way he'd daydreamed it!

He didn't care what Killer thought of him. It was what Lainie and Marty and his other friends thought that counted. And especially what he himself thought.

Chris Cosmillo came up to Kirby and the

others, the rest of his team behind him. "Ready for our game?" he asked.

"Are you sure you want to play?" Kirby asked. "I mean, even with the ref, things got awfully rough out there."

"Yeah, that's true," Chris acknowledged. "But you're forgetting one thing — we don't have to play the Bad Boys, because you guys beat them!"

"Good point!" Kirby crowed. "We did it! We finally beat the Bad Boys!"

The second game was action-packed, just like the first — except that it was a lot more fun. Chris and his teammates were good players, but they weren't any rougher than the E Street Skates. It was a contest of skating speed and hockey skills instead.

The crowd was eating it up — literally. By halftime, all the lemonade and cookies were gone! That meant they'd have enough money to pay Clayton Brown not only for next week but for the rest of the summer, too.

By the second half, the day had grown swelteringly hot as the afternoon sun broiled down on the asphalt of the rink. The Skates, playing their second game in a row, began showing the effects of all the energy they'd expended. Suddenly the Rocky Raccoons were outracing them to the puck and outskating them down the rink.

The final score was 5–3, Rocky Raccoons, much to the dismay of the hometown crowd. But as the teams were shaking hands, Chris said, "Don't worry, we know you guys were tired out from the first game. So how about we come back next week and give you a rematch?"

"Thanks," Marty said gratefully. "You guys played great. But we're going to beat you next week."

"What about the Bad Boys?" Chris asked.

"They'll just have to sit on the sidelines and wait to play the winners," Marty answered with a grin.

Someone's parents had run to the store and come back with sports drinks for all the hot, sweaty players. They skated over to the snack table and thirstily gulped them down.

"You know," Chris said to Marty and Kirby, "we've got a team we play with over in Bakersville, called the Hot Rods. They're pretty good. Do you think we could invite them over here next week? Your rink here is way better than ours, and that way we could have a real tournament — the two winners play each other. What do you think?"

"That's a fantastic idea!" Kirby said.

"Outstanding!" Marty agreed. "Bring them on — we'll play anybody, as long as they play fair and square."

"We're tired of playing the Bad Boys anyway," Trevor said, skating up to them. "With a referee, they can't beat us. No way."

Marty threw an arm around his shoulders. "Quit bragging, you fool," he told his buddy. "You know it's not true. And it wouldn't be any fun playing them if it was."

Just then, Kirby's parents called out for attention. "Everybody back to our house for ice cream!" they yelled, and the ten or so people left at the rink all cheered.

The following week's tournament was a smash, with the Skates winning it all by beating both the Rocky Raccoons and the Hot Rods (who had whipped the Bad Boys, 6–0!).

The success of the event gave Kirby an idea, and he broached it to his teammates afterward. "Why not try to start a real league?" he said. "Summer is almost over, and the rest of the kids in town will be coming back from camp soon. Why don't we get a league going for the fall? That way, we can keep on playing new teams until it starts snowing, and then start right up again in the spring."

"Great idea!" Lainie said, grinning from ear to ear. "Just so long as you make it coed all the way. Every team has to have at least two girls on it."

"What?!" Trevor cried out. But the others overruled him.

"We're not playing without Lainie," Marty pointed out. "And she's not playing if the league isn't coed."

"Um, just one thing," Nick piped up. "Who's going to tell Killer and Spike that they have to add girls or they're not in?"

Lainie laughed out loud. "Leave that to me!" she said.

No sooner said than done. The E Street Skates went right to work, using all the skills they'd learned during their petition and fund-raising drives.

By the time school started a month later, the new league was in full swing. There were two new members of the E Street Skates, since every team now had eight players (at least two of them girls). There were six teams in the league, and new ones lining up to join after the winter.

School was back in session, but Saturdays were now hockey days. The one ref had been increased to a ref and two linesmen. There were aluminum risers, donated by the town, which could seat up to one hundred spectators. (These had been a pet project of the mayor, who was now running for reelection.)

As for Kirby, he didn't think about Minford much anymore. His new life and his new friends in Valemont made him very happy. He even liked his new school. His teachers were nice, and lots of people wanted to be friends with him. In fact, he was now so popular that he had trouble finding time to be alone!

After all, he was kind of famous. He and Marty and the other E Street Skates were the celebrities of the new league. And why not? They were its founding members!

As for the Bad Boys, there would be another game coming up with them soon. It was a rivalry that would go on and on. Kirby knew that his team would win some and lose some. But that didn't bother him. He knew that was the way it was supposed to be.

One evening, after supper, his dad went into the pantry and came out with a gift box. "Kirby," he said, "this is for you, from Mom and me. We wanted to do this for you during the summer, but we decided to wait until the new league was in full swing. Here. You've earned these."

Kirby took the box and opened it up. To his amazement, inside was a brand-new pair of specially designed hockey skates!

"Mom! Dad! I can't believe this — these must have cost a fortune! You shouldn't have —"

"Never mind that," his mom said, giving him a hug and a kiss. "You've proven to us that you have what it takes to succeed."

"Not just as a hockey player, either," his dad added. "As a whole person. You've taken hits and gotten back up; you've overcome lots of obstacles. You've got grit, son. Grit and courage."

"And ingenuity, too," his mom said proudly, stroking Kirby's hair back and straightening his glasses. "Not only have you stuck with your chosen sport, but you've helped create a rink and a real hockey league!"

"I told you guys in-line hockey was a great sport," Kirby said with a grin.

"Well, it is a little rougher than I feel comfortable about," his mother said, wincing. "But it isn't all that terrible. Besides, you've given your father and me a new respect for the game."

"That's right," his dad said. "After all — it's helped our son grow up."

Kirby stood there, between the two people he loved most in the world, with his new skates before him on the table, and all his new friends to call up to spread the good news.

"Boy," he said, "I feel like the luckiest kid alive!"

Roller Hockey Associations

If you would like to learn more about in-line roller hockey, contact:

USA Hockey In-Line Hotline
1775 Bob Johnson Drive
Colorado Springs, CO 80906
tel. (719) 576-8724
http://www.USAH@usahockey.org

Roller Hockey International
13070 Fawn Hill Drive
Grass Valley, CA 95945
tel. (916) 272-7825
http://www.rollerhockey.com

Teams in the Roller Hockey League

Chicago Roller Hockey
7 Happy Road, Suite 8
Northfield, IL 60093
tel. (847) 446-1400

Denver DareDevils
1050 17th Street, #1500
Denver, CO 80215
tel. (303) 796-2600

Empire State Cobras
1 Civic Center Plaza
Glens Falls, NY 12801
tel. (518) 798-0816

Long Island Jawz
100 Ring Road West, Suite 211
Garden City, NJ 11530
tel. (201) 507-8505

Minnesota Arctic Blast
3800 First Bank Plaza
P.O. Box 357
Minneapolis, MN 55440
tel. (612) 452-3712

Oakland Skates
Worldwide Roller Hockey Facilities
12526 High Bluff Drive, Suite 210
San Diego, CA 92130
tel. (619) 259-6525

Oklahoma Coyotes
No Address Available
tel. (212) 480-2507/(800)445-6749

Philadelphia Bulldogs
Core States Spectrum
3601 South Broad Street
Philadelphia, PA 19148
tel. (215) 389-9435

Salt Lake City Sundogs
2102 East 3300 South
Salt Lake City, UT 84119
tel. (801) 487-8988

San Diego Barracudas
1743 South Douglas Road,
    Suite F
Anaheim, CA 92806
tel. (714) 385-1769

Vancouver Voodoo
Orca Bay Sports Group
800 Griffiths Way
Vancouver, BC, Canada V6B 6G1
tel. (604) 899-4604

Matt Christopher

Sports Bio Bookshelf

Terrell Davis

John Elway

Julie Foudy

Wayne Gretzky

Ken Griffey Jr.

Mia Hamm

Grant Hill

Derek Jeter

Randy Johnson

Michael Jordan

Lisa Leslie

Tara Lipinski

Mark McGwire

Greg Maddux

Hakeem Olajuwon

Briana Scurry

Sammy Sosa

Tiger Woods

Steve Young

The #1 Sports Series for Kids

Read them all!

Pressure Play

Prime-Time Pitcher

Red-Hot Hightops

The Reluctant Pitcher

Return of the Home Run Kid

Roller Hockey Radicals

Run, Billy, Run

Shoot for the Hoop

Shortstop from Tokyo

Skateboard Renegade

Skateboard Tough

Snowboard Maverick

Snowboard Showdown

Soccer Duel

Soccer Halfback

Soccer Scoop

Spike It!

The Submarine Pitch

Supercharged Infield

The Team That Couldn't Lose

Tennis Ace

Tight End

Too Hot to Handle

Top Wing

Touchdown for Tommy

Tough to Tackle

Wheel Wizards

Wingman on Ice

The Year Mom Won the Pennant

All available in paperback from Little, Brown and Company